All rights reserved. No part of this book may be reproduced in any form or b
information, s
writing from th

ISBN NO.

First Edition
Published by Taylor and Seale Publishing, LLC
© Copyright 2013

Cover and page layout by White Rabbit Graphix.

i

Rise and Shine Rosie is dedicated to all children whose home life is less than desirable, to my many friends who encouraged me to write this book, and especially to Deanna Rose, a determined child who set and achieved her goals in the face of overwhelming challenges.

Rise And Shine Rosie

Mary Kay Pyles

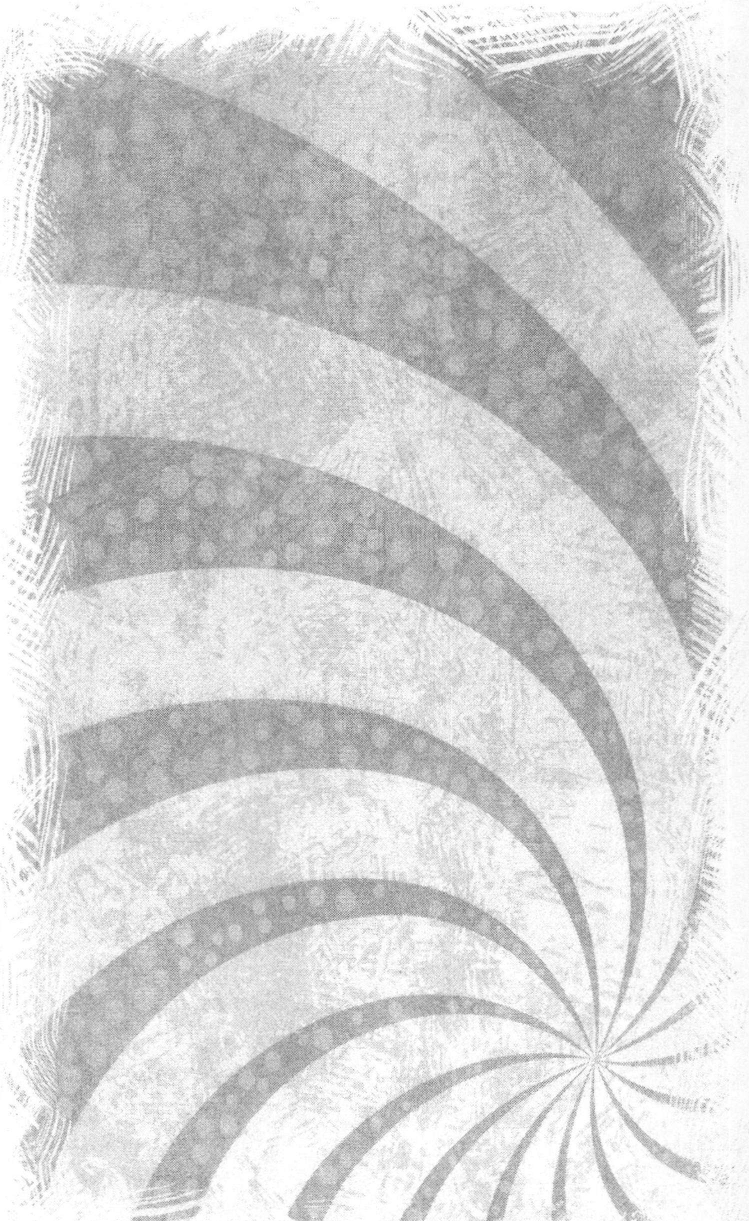

Chapter 1

Trouble at Midnight

At midnight, the air is hot and muggy. I peel my sweat-soaked shirt away from my body, flapping it up and down to create a little breeze. The only fan in our apartment is in the living room, so I decided all four of us kids would sleep there. I'm out on the front patio waiting for the twins to doze off because I can't sleep while they're still awake.

In the evening, I like to sit in the old rocking chair I rescued from the curb when the Johnsons moved away. It's a good thinking place. I have a lot to think about. Mostly, I think about Mama.

For as long as I can remember, she's worked in the housekeeping department at the Hotel Royale. She didn't finish high school, but she got her GED. For a while, she went to the community college after she got off work. We used to sit at the kitchen table and do our homework together. I felt close to her then.

Sometimes, she'd see me watching her and say, "Get busy, Baby Doll. Your job is to learn all you can while you've got the chance. Education is important. That's one thing no one can take from you."

"Mama," I asked her once. "What are you studying to be?"

"I'd like to be a hotel manager someday. I don't know if I'll make it or not, but mostly I want to provide a better life for you kids. I'd like to move you out of the projects."

She was happy back then. I wonder what changed her.

I guess I'd better introduce myself. I'm Deanna Rose Blakely. I'm eleven and I live in the Golden Oaks government housing project in Jacksonville, Florida, with my mom, Glennie Brown; my twelve-year-old brother, Calvin Thompson; and the four-year old twins, Anthony and Sophie Brown.

You may wonder why an eleven-year old is sitting out on the patio alone at night. Well, I'm not supposed to be here. Mama sometimes goes out at night and leaves me in charge. She always tells me to stay inside and lock the door. Tonight, I wish I had listened to her.

I'm sitting here, lost in thought, when I hear footsteps not ten feet away. I stop rocking, frozen in silence, hoping I won't be noticed in the darkness. Mostly, I hope no one tells Mama I'm out here this late at night.

The footsteps come closer.

A white man steps onto our patio. I gasp and spring for the door but he's faster than I am. He steps in front of me, blocking my way.

"Hey girl, what's your hurry? Where's your mama?"

I stifle a scream while I search for an answer that won't tell him we kids are here alone. No words come out. I'm so scared, I'm sure he can hear my heart pounding.

"Girl, I'm talkin' to you," he snarls, grabbing my arm roughly. "Is your mama home?"

"Don't touch me!" I yell, hoping I'll wake the neighbors. No lights come on so I guess they don't hear.

"I ain't askin' you again. You don't answer, I'll go see for myself. If she ain't here, I may take a little insurance with me."

Insurance. Somehow, I know that means me.

"J-j-just a minute," I stammer. "Sh-she's asleep. I'll go get her."

Letting go of me, he reaches for the door. I slip in ahead of him, slam the door shut, and lock it. As fast as I can, I grab a chair and stick it under the doorknob like Mama showed us. That might keep him out long enough for me to decide what to do.

"Girl, open this door now!" he yells, first rattling the doorknob, then banging the door with his fist.

Calvin, who has been sitting in the dark watching TV, jumps likes he's been shot. "What's going on, Sis? Who's out there? Are you OK?"

Calvin's a year older than I am. He's sweet, but he doesn't think real well under pressure, so I know it's up to me to get us out of this.

"Calvin, quick! Hide the twins under my bed behind the storage box."

Bam! Bam! With each blow of the man's fist on the door, my heart leaps wildly.

Clamping my hand over Sophie's mouth to keep her from screaming, I shake her awake. Calvin does the same with Anthony.

"Sophie, Anthony, go with Calvin now! I'll be right there."

The twins' eyes widen in fear, but they do as they're told.

The family pictures bounce off the wall, scattering glass everywhere when the man rams into the door. I hear the rotted doorframe splintering. It won't last long.

I've got to hurry. Rushing to the kitchen, I unlock the door and open it wide. Maybe, just maybe, he'll think we've run out the back door.

Cr-r-a-c-k! The doorframe begins to give way.

"Girl, I'm coming in!" he shouts.

Please, God, let the neighbors hear him.

I race to my bedroom and wriggle under the bed just as he crashes through the door.

We lie squeezed in like two pairs of spoons, Calvin holding Anthony, and me holding Sophie. I can feel the th-thump, th-thump of Sophie's heart—or is it mine? Sophie's shaking and her tears dampen my arms. I'm proud of her, though. She doesn't make a sound. Neither does Anthony.

The intruder curses loudly when he trips over the chair that had been braced against the door. We listen breathlessly as he stumbles through our living room. A beam of light under my bedroom door tells me that he has found the light switch.

"Where'd that brat go?" he mutters, banging open the door to each bedroom. At last, he comes to mine. When he sees no one, he goes crazy. "Stupid kid," he grumbles. He opens the closet door and begins tossing my clothes out.

"I know you're here, somewhere. When I find you, you'll be sorry you ever messed with me!"

I stifle a gasp as he lifts the bedspread. Seeing the storage box, he drops the spread and heads to the kitchen.

"Oh, man!" he yells. "That blasted kid is gone! Now what!" He says a lot of other things I won't quote. Mama would half kill me if I did.

The cupboard doors bang open and shut. What is he looking for?

We lie motionless listening to cupboard doors being slammed and chairs being tossed.

We hear police sirens approaching. The man must have heard them too because there is no sound in the house. Has he gone or is he hiding?

We stay frozen in place until we hear Mrs. Adams talking to the police. She's Aleshia Jean's grandmother. AJ's mother works in Atlanta so AJ lives with Mrs. Adams. I think they take care of each other. AJ's two years older than I am, but she's my best friend. I can trust her never to tell anyone what I tell her, and I tell her a lot.

I hear Mrs. Adams say, "I was sitting out getting some air when I saw this man come up on the patio. Then I saw Deanna Rose jump up and go into the house. After that, the banging started. I knew he was up to no good as soon as I saw him. I mean, what does a white man want in the projects in the middle of the night? They don't even come here in the daytime. That's why I called you. Oh my, I wonder what's happened to that poor child!"

"Can you give me a description, Ma'am?" the officer asks.

"Oh, yes. She's a pretty little thing. Has sparkling, dark brown eyes that seem to laugh all the time. She's a little over five feet tall, but she's growed a bit in the last year. She might be even taller. Nice straight teeth, too. Except for the little chip in one of her front teeth. The other kids are real cute, too."

I realize she's describing me.

"Ma'am, the intruder. What did he look like?"

"Oh, him? He must have gone out the back when he heard you coming. Those poor children must be scared to death with their mother gone. I wonder where she is."

How does Mrs. Adams know Mama is gone? I hope she keeps her mouth shut about how often we're left alone. Unlike AJ, she sometimes talks too much.

"Mrs. Adams, we need to find him in case he has the children. What does he look like?" the officer asks again.

"I already told you, he's white. It's midnight. I couldn't see all the details from across the street. He has on dark pants and a dark shirt. I think that's odd, it being so hot and all. I mean, don't folks usually wear lighter clothes when it's hot?" Mrs. Adams rambles on.

I step out onto the patio.

"O-o-h child! Are you okay?" Mrs. Adams, smelling of sautéed onions, freshly baked bread, and the lavender perfume she always wears, nearly hugs the breath out of me.

"We're fine," I manage to say when she finally quits squeezing me.

"Who are you?" the officer asks.

"I'm Deanna Rose Blakely. I live here."

"I'm Sergeant Harris. Can you tell me what happened?"

I tell him about the guy breaking down the door,

but leave out the part about Mama being gone.

"Can you describe him?" Sergeant Harris asks.

"Yes, he has light blond hair and he was wearing an Atlanta Braves baseball hat."

"Anything else? How tall is he?"

"He's a little taller than you. Oh, yes, he was wearing glasses with wire frames and he has a long, jagged scar on his right wrist. I saw it when he grabbed me. That's all I remember."

I'm trying my best to be helpful, all the while hoping he doesn't ask to speak to Mama.

He doesn't have to. At that moment, his partner comes out of the apartment with Calvin, Anthony, and Sophie.

"Hey, Sarge," he announces. "Look what I found. Doesn't look like their mama's home. I guess we'll have to take them with us. We can't let them stay here with a maniac running around, breaking into people's houses."

"We'll be all right," I protest. "Mama will be back any minute. Auntie Grace is sick and Mama went to check on her." I have no idea where she really is and I know it's wrong to lie, but I don't want us to be gone when Mama gets home.

"Listen," Sergeant Harris pauses to look for my name in his notes, "Deanna, I can't leave you here. We'll take you kids with us and find a place for you to stay. Mrs. Adams, will you please tell their mother to check at the police station when she gets home?"

"That won't be necessary," I hear my grandfather say from the darkness as he approaches the house. "I just got a call that my grandbabies are having a little trouble. I'll look after them."

Chapter 2

Papa Joe

Papa Joe is tall and frail, almost rickety, and he wheezes when he breathes. I think it's from all the smoking he used to do. He looks like he can hardly take care of himself, much less four children, but he's strong inside. When he says he'll do something, people just naturally know he will. I think that's why the police don't question him when he says he'll take care of us. Either that, or they notice how all of us gather around him like we trust him.

When they leave, Papa Joe tips his cap to Mrs. Adams. I guess, in the old days, that was the polite thing to do. "Thank you, Ma'am, for calling me."

"Humph," she grunts, turning toward her home. "Probably shouldn't have."

Papa Joe stares after her quizzically, then herds us into our dingy duplex.

"What on earth happened here?" he demands, looking at the splintered doorframe and broken furniture.

"Someone lookin' for Mama broke in," I answer.

Usually Papa Joe's eyes have a twinkle to them, but now they look hard and angry and his jaws are clenched. He's more upset than I've ever seen him.

"Rosie," he says sternly. He calls me Rosie because I was named after my Grandma Rose. "You and

Calvin put the twins to bed; then we'll talk."

Usually, I love to talk with Papa Joe, but tonight his voice is cold and distant.

While we settle Sophie and Anthony into their beds, Calvin whispers, "You talk. I'm going to sleep."

"Calvin, that's not fair!" I protest, but Calvin has already disappeared. I love my brother, but he's a master at ducking out during a crisis.

Back in the kitchen, Papa Joe is sitting at the table with his long, gangly legs stretched out and his cane hooked over a chair.

At first, neither of us says anything. The silence is loud and uncomfortable.

Finally, he says, "Rosie Girl, how'd I come to have a daughter I don't know about?"

I don't expect this question. "What do you mean?" I ask, forgetting my lie to the police.

"I mean, how often does your Mama visit your sick Auntie Grace?"

Papa Joe will be furious with Mama if I tell the truth and disappointed in me if I lie, so I stare at the floor without answering.

He puts his gnarled fingers under my chin and tilts my head to look at him.

"Rosie," he says gently. "I asked you a question."

"Every once in a while," I answer.

He can tell I'm not going to rat on Mama, so he changes the subject abruptly.

"I make a pretty mean scrambled egg sandwich," he says. "How about I make you a midnight snack? Then we'll get this mess cleaned up."

"I'm not hungry, Papa Joe." The truth is I haven't

eaten all day, but there's nothing in the refrigerator but a little milk, a half loaf of bread, and a can of Mama's beer.

"Well, I am," he declares, opening the refrigerator door. He stares at the empty shelves, then slowly turns to look at me. "Deanna Rose, when was the last time you ate?"

"We usually eat around 6:00." I'm good at giving vague, misleading answers, but Papa Joe sees right through this one.

"Rosie, I know you love your mama and she loves you, but sometimes parents don't do what's right by their children. When that happens, you've got to talk to someone. I can't help unless I know."

I desperately want to tell him about our being left alone and about how hungry we are, but I can't betray Mama. I lower my head to hide my tears, but when he hugs me close to him, I can't keep them in any longer. I feel so safe and cared for with Papa Joe's arms around me. He lets me cry without asking any more questions.

Finally, I ask, "Papa Joe, can you stay here with us?"

"I'll stay 'til your mama gets home," he answers gruffly. "You go on to bed."

I'm awakened before dawn by the sound of voices in the kitchen.

"What are you doing here?" Mama asks.

"Lookin' out for your babies. Where've you been?"

"Out," Mama answers defiantly.

Uh-oh, Mama's in one of her moods.

"Glennie," Papa Joe scolds, "you ain't actin' right. Look at this mess. If it hadn't been for Rosie's quick thinking and the police coming when they did, there's no telling what might have happened!"

"Police!" Mama screeched. "Why were they here?"

"Near as I can tell, Mrs. Adams called 'em when she saw some white man chase Rosie into the house."

At that, Mama comes unglued.

"Deanna Rose, get out here this minute," she screams, pounding on my door. There's no sense pretending to be asleep. When Mama gets upset, you can't ignore her.

"Leave Rosie out of this," Papa Joe says, but Mama keeps ranting.

"Deanna Rose, haven't I told you to stay inside and lock the door when I'm gone?"

"Yes," I mumble.

"Yes, what?"

"Yes, Mama."

She raises her hand to hit me, but Papa Joe grabs it.

"Glennie, don't. If you'd been here, this wouldn't have happened."

Mama gives him a look of pure hatred before slamming her bedroom door shut behind her.

Papa Joe opens his arms and once again, I melt into them.

"I'm so scared," I tell him. "I don't know what's happening to Mama, but it's not good."

I can feel Papa Joe's heart beating rapidly, but his voice is calm. "Rosie Girl, try to get some sleep. Things

12

always look better in the morning."
 I go back to bed, but I can't sleep. I'm scared. Mothers aren't supposed to change like mine did.

Chapter 3

An Unwanted Discovery

Sunlight streams into my room between the slats of the tattered venetian blinds. I lie with my eyes closed not wanting to face the day, but Sophie is wide-awake. She crawls up beside my face, and, with her delicate little fingers, pushes my eyelids up.

"Are you awake, Rosie?" she asks innocently. She is so cute I have to laugh.

"I'm hungry," she says.

I toast the last of the bread and pour milk over it for breakfast for the three of us. I have no idea when we'll eat again.

Calvin has already gone.

Mama doesn't like to be disturbed, so I leave a note that I'm taking the twins to the Golden Oaks Playground. They race to the kiddie slide and climb the ladder, their short legs barely able to reach the next step.

"One at a time," I caution them when they reach the top. They have other ideas. Sitting one behind the other, they shove off in tandem and squeal in delight all the way to the bottom. Landing in a tangled heap, they lie there giggling, then jump up and go again. When they tire of that, they dash off to the jungle gym. Finally, they wear themselves out. That's good. Maybe I'll get a chance to visit with my best friend, AJ, while they sleep.

We're almost home when I see AJ motioning to me from her back stoop. It's good to see her again. She's been in Atlanta visiting her mom the last two weeks.

"Ooh, Girl," she whispers, talking low so the twins won't hear, "your mama's been throwing a fit. She's been screaming and yelling and she told your granddad not to come aroun' no more. She said she didn't need help taking care of her kids."

"B-but he was already gone when I left, " I stammer.

"Well, she lit into him when he came back with groceries. I think the whole neighborhood heard her."

I can't think of anything worse than not being able to see Papa Joe. I sink down onto the porch and bury my head in my hands. I feel like my guardian angel has been snatched away.

"What's going on, Rosie?" AJ asks, settling down beside me. I shake my head. I can't tell her. If she ever let it slip that Mama is gone most of the time, we'd really be in trouble. No, it's best to deal with it myself.

"Rosie, why don't you come over tonight when your mama gets off work? I'll tell you all about my trip to Atlanta."

"I'll ask," I promise.

Mama worked the afternoon shift today so she's late getting home. The twins love to watch for her bus. They have this game of racing to the bus stop to see who can hug her first. Usually she hugs them back, but not tonight.

"Stop it!" she snaps, pushing them away from her with such force that Sophie stumbles off the sidewalk.

"Mama!" I scream, racing toward the street. "Mama!

A car's coming!"

Mama's in her own world. She's oblivious to the honking horn, the squealing brakes, and my screams. Fortunately, I reach Sophie before the car does and snatch her out of harm's way.

I sit on the curb hugging the sobbing twins. I'm glad they're safe, but I'm furious with Mama. They love her so much, and they don't deserve to be treated like this. Matter of fact, none of us deserves Mama's treatment lately. I don't understand her and, the truth is, I don't much like her when she's this way.

"Mama," I say, careful to keep my tone respectful, "what's wrong? Sophie was almost killed, but you just walked away."

She looks at me, her eyes dark and dull.

"Baby," she said, "I've got a terrible headache. Take the twins to your room and keep 'em quiet. I can't take their noise tonight."

If thoughts could kill, she'd be dead. I've been watching the twins all day and I want to go see AJ. I know better than to say what I'm thinking.

"Come on, y'all," I say to the twins. On the way to my room, I notice something new. Way up at the top of the door, there's a hook and eye latch. I know in my bones Mama is going to lock us in. I wish more than ever that I hadn't been out on the patio last night.

Sure enough, I hear the latch click behind us. I'm afraid, more afraid than I have ever been. It's bad enough when someone else breaks into your house, but when you're not safe with your own mother, that's really scary.

The twins finally stop whimpering and fall asleep.

I'm wide-awake. Calvin's not home yet, Mama's acting weird, and I'm locked in. Any one of those is enough to keep me awake.

I have a silly little clock that looks like a pair of lips. Every hour, the lips start moving and tell the time. I'm still awake when the clock tells me it's 1:00. I'm not prepared for what I hear next.

Mama is talking in a low whisper. "You're a fool, Kyle, for comin' here. You ever threaten my children again, it's the last thing you'll do."

I creep stealthily to the door. There's a good-sized crack between the door and the frame where I can peek out. I can't believe what I'm seeing. That same white man who tore up our house last night is sitting at the table talking with Mama!

"Shut up, Glennie. I wasn't going to hurt your darlin' little angel. I was just going to take her until you came through. You got the stuff?"

Mama nods. From her pocket, she pulls out some little bags of white powder and puts them on the table.

Kyle opens a bag, dips his finger in, touches it to his lips, and nods.

He pulls out a wad of bills, peels some off, and tosses them on the table saying, "Next time, don't be late, or I'll find another source."

My legs turn to rubber. My stomach heaves. I break out in a sweat as waves of nausea flow through me. I grab my pillow and hold it over my mouth, partly to hold in the scream I feel throughout my whole body and partly to keep from throwing up. My mother – a drug dealer! My mother who always told us not to touch the stuff!

17

Chapter 4

Convincing Calvin

I can't sleep. I feel like I'm alone in a deep, dark hole. I know Mama's secret, but wish with all my heart I didn't. The drugs explain her mood swings and the lock on my door, but nothing explains the drugs. Why is my mother, who has always warned us about drugs, selling them? What happened to her dream of managing a hotel? I lie awake, trying to sort it all out.

Finally, the long night is over. I start for the bathroom, forgetting the door is still locked. I turn the handle. The door doesn't open. Panicking, I yank it again and again. It doesn't budge. Anger and frustration well up inside me. Somehow, I've got to get out without waking the twins. The last thing I need is for them to start crying. I dress quickly, quietly unlatch the screen, and crawl out the window. When I get to the kitchen, Calvin is already there.

"Where've you been?" he asks.

"Locked in," I answer, reaching up to unlatch the door.

His eyes widen. "Wh-when did that get there?" he sputters.

I shrug. "I dunno. Yesterday, I guess."

"Calvin," I whisper, "we have to talk."

"About what?"

"Later," I answer hurriedly when I hear Mama

opening her bedroom door.

I feel so betrayed I can hardly stand to look at her. How can she sit here eating breakfast as if everything is normal? When the twins get up, she gives them each a big hug. They break into wide smiles, seeming to forget how she treated them last night.

"Deanna," she says, "Look after the twins today. I'm working late tonight. No tellin' what time I'll get home."

Oh, man, I think. What about me? I'm just a kid myself. I want to visit my friends and do regular kid things. I love the twins, but they're your babies, not mine. Of course, I don't say any of those things. Instead, I answer obediently, "Yes, Mama."

Calvin heads out the door as soon as Mama leaves, but I catch him before he gets away. "Calvin, I'm taking the twins to the park and I need you to come with me."

"No way! Babysittin' is girl stuff!" he says adamantly.

"Listen Calvin, we have to talk where the twins can't hear us. Now come on."

Grudgingly, he tags along.

"Okay, what's so important?" he demands when the twins race off through the park.

"I found out why Mama's been acting so strange. Calvin, you won't believe this, but she's into drugs."

Instantly, he is screaming in my face.

"You liar! Mama wouldn't do that."

"Calvin, listen! I saw her!"

"No! No! No! I won't listen to your lies!" he shouts, stalking away.

That worked well, didn't it? Now, I'm more alone than ever. Maybe he'll eventually come around, but right now he can't handle the truth.

The truth begins to dawn on him when he sees that there's a latch on his door, too, and when Mama doesn't come home that night or the next.

Chapter 5

Social Services

Sunday morning, when I get up, Mama is slumped over the kitchen table, her chin resting on her hands. Her coffee cup sits untouched beside her. She looks like she might be crying.

"Mama," I ask gently, "are you all right?"

I'm still angry with her, but, at the same time, I feel sorry for her and I'm glad she's back home. I miss the mama she once was.

She stiffens up. "I'm fine, just fine."

"I thought you were crying. Mama, do you think we could go to church today?"

Mama rolls her eyes upward. "Why?" is all she says.

I'm thinking maybe the preacher will talk about how using drugs is wrong and Mama will remember what she used to teach us, but all I say is, "Back when we used to go, you were happier."

"Humph! Ain't gonna do me no good to go," she snorts. "Your mama's missed the happiness boat."

"But Mama," I protest, "you used to say that we should try to be happy. Remember, every day when you'd wake me up, you'd say, 'Rise and shine, Rosie. Make today a good day.'"

Mama nods, remembering. Her mouth turns up with an inkling of a smile.

I feel like I'm the mama, encouraging her child, instead of the other way around.

Our conversation is interrupted by a knock on the door. Mama's smile quickly fades and her eyes narrow with suspicion--or is it fear?

"Mrs. Brown?" a lady inquires, holding up her ID card, "I'm Shirley Walker from social services. May I come in?"

Mama's face turns dark and inscrutable. She opens the door and stands to one side.

Ms. Walker sweeps in, looking very official. "I hate to bother you on a Sunday morning, but I'm checking out a hotline call we received that your children have been left alone for the past several days."

"Does it look like they're alone?" Mama's voice is stone cold.

"No, Ma'am, not right now," Ms. Walker answers. "I'm sure you understand we have to follow up on every call."

Mama says nothing.

"It's very dangerous to leave children alone," Ms. Walker continues.

Mama stares at her without responding.

I know Mama. She's going to stand there and say absolutely nothing until Ms. Walker leaves.

"Mrs. Brown, I'm leaving now, but if we get another call, I'll have to come back. If we find that the reports are true, we'll have to consider putting your children in foster homes."

Mama still says nothing. Instead, she glowers at Ms. Walker.

Finally, Ms. Walker gets the hint. "Well, here's my

card," she says. "If you need anything, call me."

I smile to myself. Right, I think. You come in here investigating and threatening, then give Mama your card. It'll be in the trashcan before the door is shut behind you.

Ms. Walker hasn't even reached the sidewalk when Mama whirls to face me.

"Deanna Rose Blakely, did you call social services? If you did--,"

"No, Mama." Backing away, I cut her off in midsentence. "I didn't, honest!"

"Well," she says, "Well, well, well. If you didn't, it was probably that nosy Mrs. Adams. Have you been talking to AJ?"

"I haven't talked to anyone. I've been right here watching Sophie and Anthony the whole time. We've been either here or at the playground every day."

"The playground, huh? Mrs. Adams probably saw you go and figured you were alone. That's it!" she says decisively. "From now on, you'll stay home with the doors locked. No more playground!"

"But, Mama, we go to the playground when you're home. If Mrs. Adams is the one who called and she doesn't see us going to the playground, she'll know something's wrong."

Mama rants on. "And another thing," she says, "you keep the blinds pulled so Ms. High and Mighty Walker can't see in if she comes back."

I try again. "Mama, it's dark in here and it's hot."

"And furthermore," she continues, "if anyone comes to the door, you're not to let them in. Not anyone. You hear me?"

"I hear you," I sigh. Shutting us in is worse abuse than leaving us alone. We'll be prisoners in our own home.

Tentatively, I ask, "Mama, why don't you just come home? That way, we'll be back to normal."

Her eyes narrow to small slits. "Girl, are you questioning your mama?"

Of course, I'm questioning you, my brain screams. I have a right to some answers. Aloud, I say, "Of course not, Mama."

Chapter 6

Summer Challenges

It's Thursday morning and Mama has been home every evening since Ms. Walker's visit. She must be afraid of being checked on again. She usually sleeps until she goes to work, but at least she's here. I'm over at AJ's for the first time all week when I hear Mama calling, "Deanna! Deanna Rose Blakely!" When she calls me by my whole name, I know to hurry. I'm home in thirty seconds flat.

"Girl, I thought I told you to stay home!" She's in one of her moods.

"You did," I try to explain, "but I thought that was just for when you're not here."

"It's for all the time unless I say different! Suppose something had happened to Sophie or Anthony while I was asleep?"

From her tone of voice, I can tell she's in an argumentative mood. I know I can't win, so I keep quiet.

"Here." She thrusts a list and some loose change in my hand. "We need groceries."

When I see Cool Longs, Mama's favorite cigarettes, at the top of the list, I know I don't have enough money. I also know I'd better not come home without the Cool Longs.

The only three food items on the list are cereal, milk, and bread. The bad thing is, we're totally out of food and our food stamps aren't due for another eight days.

I haven't gone far when I hear a little voice. "Take me, Rosie. Take me."

Sophie is trudging along behind me, trying her best to catch up.

"Sophie, I can't. It's way too far for you to walk, and I can't carry both you and the groceries. Besides, there are a lot of cars and I don't want you to get run over. Now, go on home."

All those reasons are true, but the real reason is this is my time to be alone with God. He and I have a wonderful relationship. I often talk to Him when I'm alone. He never answers me out loud, but I always feel like He's close by, watching over me. It's a good thing He is because no one else seems to care.

Today, I talk to Him about Mama. "God," I say, ""Why doesn't Mama love us anymore? I don't ask for much, but we need Mama to care about us again and we need food."

Don't misunderstand me. I know God won't drop those things down from heaven just because I ask for them. I remember, though, that the preacher said one Sunday we should tell God what we need. He said that when we talk to God, it helps us see things differently. To tell the truth, I don't know how you can see hunger differently. If you're hungry, you're hungry.

To get to the store, I have to cross a six-lane highway with a concrete median. While waiting for the pedestrian walk signal, I notice something that looks like money wadded up at the edge of the median. When the cars finish whizzing by, I step off the curb and
26

snatch it up. Sure enough, it's a twenty-dollar bill. My first thought is that God has answered my prayer, but then I remember I didn't pray for money. Besides, God certainly didn't send twenty dollars floating down to the median. It doesn't matter to me how it got there. What matters is that I have enough money to get everything on the list, plus some fruit and potatoes.

When I get home, I race into Mama's bedroom where she's dressing to go out. "Look, Mama!" I shout gleefully. "I found a twenty-dollar bill. I got everything on the list and have seven dollars left over." I'm so excited my words spill out. "Now we'll have enough money to last until the first of the month."

She glares at me coldly, lights a cigarette, holds out her hand and snaps her fingers impatiently. Reluctantly, I give her the money. Stuffing it into her handbag, she leaves, calling over her shoulder, "I'll be back. Y'all watch the twins."

Calvin and I look at each other despondently. My spirit shrivels and a dull, aching bitterness replaces my excitement. It may be days before Mama is back.

Saturday morning, I'm awakened by Anthony's ear-piercing screams.

"Anthony, what's wrong?"

"My ear hurts. Make it stop!"

I hug him close and comfort him while I try to think of what Mama would do. Maybe warm water will help.

I call for Calvin to get me a washcloth with warm water and I hold it to Anthony's ear. The warmth doesn't help much and Anthony screams even louder, "Where's Mama! I want Mama!"

Sophie, frightened by Anthony's screams, starts

crying, too. "Mama! I want Mama!"

"Mama's on vacation," I tell them. "I'm not sure when she'll be back." I hope God forgives me for lying. It's the best thing I can think to say at the moment. There's no way four-year-olds would understand the truth. I don't understand it myself. Besides, it's not a total lie. She is on vacation from being a mother and I'm not sure when she'll be back.

Every time I take the washcloth off to warm it up again, Anthony screams. Sophie joins in, not in pain, but because she doesn't want to be left out. Finally, in desperation, I call out, "Calvin, go get Mrs. Adams. Ask her to hurry." I hate to do that because I know how she talks, but I can't handle two squalling children, especially when one is sick.

In a few minutes, Mrs. Adams bustles in with sweet oil and a hot water bottle.

She puts drops of sweet oil in Anthony's ear, tsk-tsking while she does. I calm Sophie down while Mrs. Adams rocks Anthony to sleep.

"Child," Mrs. Adams says, "where is your mama, and don't give me that nonsense about her going off to visit your sick Auntie Grace."

Sophie, who stopped crying when Anthony fell asleep, looks up innocently and says, "Mama's on va--." I put my hand over her mouth. If Mrs. Adams hears that Mama is on vacation, she'll have Ms. Walker here in a hot second.

"She'll be back soon," I answer.

"Humph," Mrs. Adams snorts. "I doubt that. If you ask me, I don't think you know where she is or when she'll be back."

There's no way she's going to get me to talk about Mama, even if Mama is doing wrong. As politely as possible, I say, "I really appreciate your helping with Anthony, Mrs. Adams. I think I can handle it now."

Mrs. Adams is a pretty sharp old lady and she knows when she's being dismissed, but she's not quite ready to go. She stands in the doorway with one hand on her hip and looks around. It's a good thing I keep the house clean because I get the feeling she's trying to find some reason to report us.

"Well," she says finally, "call me if you need me."

"Humph," I hear her snort again as she goes down the sidewalk. "It just ain't right how Glennie treats those children."

Three days later, Mama returns, drunk and dirty. She smells of cigarettes and booze, her hair is disheveled, and her new red dress is filthy. Disgust, resentment, and pity all mix together in my mind. Why has she done this to herself? I help her into the shower and then into bed. She sleeps most of the day.

Anthony and Sophie are so excited she's home, they can hardly wait for her to wake up. When she does, they bounce up on the bed and snuggle in beside her. It's amazing how forgiving they are. I find it hard to forgive, especially when I hear what she's saying.

She gives Anthony a big hug and says, "Sweetie, Mama heard that you and Sophie were crying the other morning. Did Deanna and Calvin do something to hurt you? If they ever do, you let Mama know."

I positively seethe with anger. How did she hear about their crying? How dare she ask if I'm mistreating them! If the twins don't trust me, there's no one they

29

can trust.

Mrs. Adams told the truth! It's not right how Mama's treating us!

Chapter 7

Eavesdropping

It's another typical summer evening. Calvin's out somewhere, the twins and I are locked in my room, and Mama is stoned on drugs. I know because I looked out the crack in the door and saw her shooting up. The twins are asleep and I'm reading The Mystery of Swallow Creek. Just as I get to a really scary part, I hear, "Psst! Psst!"

Startled, I throw the book straight up in the air and dive under my bed.

"Rosie, it's me," AJ whispers. "Can you come out?"

"No, Mama will kill me if she comes to and finds out I'm gone!"

"It's important, Rosie! It's something you have to hear." I turn off the light, lift out the screen, and slip out the window in a wink.

"What's going on?" I ask.

AJ puts her finger over her lips, motioning me to be quiet.

Stealthily, we creep to the window under Mrs. Adams' living room.

"Joe," Mrs. Adams is saying, "you've got to find a way to help those children. I sit out on my porch 'til late at night, and I know they're by themselves. Most of the time, Deanna's alone with the twins. Why, just the other day, she sent Calvin to fetch me because Anthony had a bad earache. Both of the twins was screechin' and hollerin' and callin' for their mama. Deanna won't give her mama up, but I'm telling you, it's a shame the way Glennie treats those little ones."

"I was afraid something like that was happening," Papa Joe answers. "Glennie got real mad at me when I took food by. Said she could take care of her own. Said she didn't need my help."

"Maybe she doesn't need your help, but those poor children do. Why, even when she's home, she's not doing right. She won't let the children out; she won't let Deanna visit AJ; and to top it all, she has that white man over who broke into the house that night. You've got to do something."

"Ruby, I don't know what to do. I can't keep the children because my health isn't too good. Tell you what. If you'll send word when you know they're alone, I'll come check on them."

"That'll help some, but it's not good enough. Why, I just couldn't live with myself if something happened to them and I hadn't done anything to help. I think I should call Ms. Walker again. Not that it helped the first time. I don't for the life of me know how Glennie found out she was coming, but she showed up just in time."

"Well, Ruby, think about what you just said. If Glennie's not home when Ms. Walker comes to check, she'll take the children and put them in different homes. All those children have is one another. It'd be a shame to separate them."

"That's true, Joe, but it's not fair to Deanna for her to look after the babies all the time. That child's still in grade school and she's responsible for the family like she's a grown woman. She's doing a good job, mind you, but she's got no time at all to play with her friends. She no sooner got here the other day when Glennie called her home. I think Glennie's afraid Deanna will tell AJ about her being gone so much."

I've heard enough. I crawl away from the window and motion for AJ to follow.

"How long have you known about Mama?" I ask.

"Grandma's been watching ever since the night that man broke into your house. She says it's her duty to call Ms. Walker. Says it's the law that if you know something's wrong, you have to report it."

"Listen, AJ, Papa Joe's right. We'll be separated if Ms. Walker takes us. No one wants four children. See if you can stall your grandma a bit until I figure out a plan."

Chapter 8

The Plan

I climb back through the window, replace the screen, and crawl into bed. All night, thoughts tumble through my mind as I try to figure out what to do.

There's Mama on drugs and gone for days at a time, the twins to care for, strangers coming to the house when Mama's home, Ms. Walker spying on us, Mrs. Adams threatening to report us again, and now Papa Joe's health. To top it off, school starts next week. I have no idea how to care for the twins while I'm in school. One thing I'm sure of is I want out of the projects. To do that, I have to go to school.

Shortly before daybreak, I fall asleep with the beginning of a plan in mind.

I'm startled awake by the sound of "Psst. Psst." It's AJ at the window again.

"Wake up, Girl. Unlock your door."

Groggily, I pad over to the window. "What are you doing here so early?" I mumble.

"It's 10:00, Rosie! I've got the twins. They were playing in the street. I brought them home, but we're locked out."

My mind is instantly in high gear. How did they get out? What if someone saw them? What if Mrs. Adams decided I was careless and called Ms. Walker?

Frustrated and panicky, I tug on my shorts, grab a

T-shirt, and pull it on as I race to open the door.

Sophie has the misfortune of being closest to me. I yank her into the house screeching, "Don't you ever, ever go out this door without me! Not ever again, do you understand?"

Big tears well up in her eyes and her chin quivers. Her gulping, sniffling sobs quickly become high-pitched squalls.

Seeing Sophie so upset, Anthony starts an outburst of his own. "Mama! I want Mama!" he bellows.

"Stop it, all of you!" AJ's usually calm voice rises shrilly above the din.

Startled by her sharpness, I stop yelling.

The twins inch closer to AJ as if they're afraid of me. Instinctively, I know I've crossed some invisible line between trust and fear. Somehow, I have to keep their trust. If they're afraid of me, they'll have no one to trust. I'm all they have, but they're all I have, too. I couldn't bear it if the twins no longer trusted me.

Quickly, I kneel down to hug and comfort them. "I'm so sorry. I love you. Really, I do. I yelled at you because I was scared. When AJ said you were playing in the street, I was afraid you'd get hurt."

Sophie relents first. Slowly, she stops crying and puts her sticky, sweaty arms around my neck. Watching Sophie, Anthony snuggles in close. With tears glistening on his long eye-lashes, he says, "I wuv you, too, Wosie."

"Rosie," AJ interrupts gently, "I hate to break this up, but have you thought about what you're going to do when school starts next week?"

Wordlessly, I stare at her. Mrs. Adams always says

35

that AJ and I are real soul sisters. We think on the same wavelength so often it's as if our brains were attached to each other.

Not wanting to frighten the twins, I change the subject. "Are you guys ready for some cereal?"

AJ gets the message. She waits patiently while they wolf down their breakfast, then go to the bedroom to play.

"So, have you thought about it?" she repeats when they are engrossed with their building blocks.

With more confidence than I feel, I reply, "Mama will be back. She knows I need to be in school, but if she's not, I've got a plan."

"It better be a good one, Rosie. I have a feeling you'll need it."

"I think it'll work, but I need your help with Calvin."

Puzzled, AJ asks, "What do you mean?"

"I need you to tell him how important it is for him to help. My plan won't work without him, but he's gone most of every day."

"Why would he listen to me?"

"Girl, Calvin's crazy about you! Wherever you are, you can bet he's somewhere near. He'll do anything you ask."

"Don't be silly," AJ blusters. "I'm a year older than he is and I'm two years ahead of him in school. He doesn't even know I exist."

I wonder if she really doesn't know how he idolizes her. "Oh? Then maybe you can tell me why he's always watching you and why the school picture you gave me is in his dresser drawer. He definitely knows you exist! Come over this evening when he's home. I'll tell you my plan then."

It's almost dark when AJ knocks on the door. "Anyone home?" she calls through the screen.

One look at her and I can see she has taken her job seriously. "Like my outfit?" she asks, twirling around to give the full effect. "I got it in Atlanta when I went shopping with my mom." She's wearing a white lace-up t-shirt with beads and sequins all around the eyelets. Leather laces outline the seams and pockets of her bell-bottom jeans.

She may have overdone her outfit a bit because Calvin can't stop gawking at her.

"Okay, what's the plan?" she asks, seemingly unaware of Calvin's gaze.

"What plan?" Calvin inquires.

"The plan I've figured out for taking care of the twins when school starts. If Mama's home, we'll both go to school. If she's gone, we'll have to take turns staying home. That way, neither of us will get too far behind."

"Unh-uh! No way, Sis! I'm not getting stuck with two kids every other day!"

"Calvin, think! We can't leave them here alone. If we do, Ms. Walker will find out.

She'll put us all in separate foster homes. You've got to help!" I insist.

"Calvin, they need their big brother," AJ purrs, resting her hand lightly on his arm. "If you do it, I'll come help when I get home."

Calvin's resolve melts.

"P-p-promise?" he stutters.

"I promise."

"Well, okay, I'll do it. Rosie, why don't you go the

first day?"

He's so awestruck he doesn't realize he's been snookered. AJ will come as promised, but she's in middle school and won't get home until after I do. He won't have much time alone with her.

"I've also been thinking about food, Calvin. You and I get free breakfast and lunch at school, but if Mama doesn't have groceries here, the twins won't have anything. Whichever one of us goes to school will need to save part of our meals to share with Sophie and Anthony."

"Oh, man! I'm hungry when I eat all of mine. Are you trying to starve me? Besides what are we supposed to do – put food in our pockets?"

"Calvin, stop being selfish. You're not going to starve and the twins have to eat!"

"I'll get some baggies from Granny Adams' kitchen and I'll save part of my meals too," AJ offers. "That should help a little. Besides, giving up part of my meals will keep me from getting fat."

Calvin looks at her dainty figure. "Not much chance of that," he declares.

Chapter 9

Sixth Grade Dreams and Dilemmas

"Rise and shine, Rosie! You don't want to miss the bus."

Hearing Mama's voice, I leap out of bed and run to the kitchen shouting, "Mama, you're home!" I throw my arms around her neck and give her a big hug.

"Well, I can't have my girl missing school, can I?" Mama answers.

The weight of responsibility vanishes along with my anger toward Mama. She's here today when I need her. That's all that matters.

I board the bus, feeling like a bird being let out of a cage. Funny. I think most kids feel free when they get out of school. Me? I feel free when I go back. Except for going to the grocery store, I haven't been out of the projects all summer. In fact, since Mama banned our going to the park, we've been stuck in our duplex. I can hardly wait to get to school!

At Oakland Park Elementary, class lists are posted on the courtyard walls. I join the other sixth graders, all of us jostling to find our names.

"Deanna. Deanna Rose, can you believe it! We're in the same class again!" shrieks my friend, Lakeshia Hines. Eagerly, we scan the list for other familiar names.

I'm looking for Tremayne Morris. He's my favorite

guy friend. He's not what you'd call handsome, but he's smart and funny. We have an ongoing competition to see who can get the best grades. Last year, I got three more A's than he did. Lakeshia says if I want him to like me, I should let him get more A's, but that makes no sense to me. Why should he like someone who doesn't do well?

Tyrell Williams, the class clown, is in our room too. He spends a lot of time in the office. The four of us from the Golden Oaks projects have been together nearly every year. I'm glad because we're good friends.

Our teacher, Mrs. Bass, is new to the school. At least 50 years old, she's tall and slender with short, graying hair and crisp blue eyes with little crinkly lines around them when she smiles. "Good morning," she greets each of us. "Sit where you find your name tag."

On each desk is a sheet of lined paper. Tyrell rolls his eyes and heads his paper, "What I Did On My Summer Vacation."

That, however, is not the assignment. After introducing herself, Mrs. Bass says,

"You probably think I'm going to ask you to write about your summer vacation. I'm not. Summer is past and you can't change it. Instead, I want you to write about your goals for the future. The future can be the end of this year, your middle and high school years, college, or your career."

Tyrell crumples his paper and arches it toward the wastebasket. "Two points," he announces as it wobbles on the edge and falls in.

How is she going to handle him? If she doesn't stop him now, she'll have a miserable year.

Calmly, Mrs. Bass puts another sheet of paper on Tyrell's desk. "The kind of goal I'm talking about is how you see yourself in the future. If you see yourself as a basketball star, write about that. The important thing is that you have goals and that you work toward them. You can't make a basket without shooting the ball and you can't reach goals you don't have. If you're willing to share your goals with me, I'll do my best to help you reach them."

I've never really thought about life that way. I don't want to stay in the projects; I don't want to be separated from my brothers and sister; and I don't want Mama on drugs. I can't write any of that. It says what I don't want. Besides, it's too personal. What if Mrs. Bass puts our papers on the wall and other kids see it.

I stare at the empty sheet, thinking. Ever since Mama and I used to do homework together, I've wanted to go to college, but I don't know what I want to be. Finally, I write, "I have four goals. I want to learn everything I can, stay on honor roll, earn money, and go to college."

A shadow falls across my paper. It's Mrs. Bass. She puts a hand on my shoulder and says softly, "Good goals! If you meet the first two, you could get college scholarships."

"What's a scholarship?" I ask.

"It's money to help pay college expenses."

That's all I need to hear. Seven years is a long time to keep things together at home, but I'm smart. I know I can get the grades if I really study. For the first time ever, I see the possibility of a future outside the projects.

Mrs. Bass doesn't play. I'm loaded down with homework the first night.

I expect the twins to come running to greet me when I get off the bus, but they don't. "Hello, anybody home?" I call out. "Mama? Sophie? Anthony?"

There's no answer except silence and darkness. The blinds are drawn. The lights are off. I try to tell myself they're asleep, but in my heart, I know they're gone.

I'm not sure how you can be cold and sweat at the same time, but that's what is happening. My stomach lurches. I feel like I'm going to vomit. My knees weaken and buckle. Could Ms. Walker have taken the twins? Would she be mean enough to wait for me to be gone and then snatch them away?

I drop my books on the table and race wildly from room to room searching for the twins, for Calvin, for anybody. No one is here.

Think, I tell myself. Think. Check with Mrs. Adams. If anything is wrong, she'll know. She knows everything that happens on the block.

My feet feel like lead weights as I cross the street.

Mrs. Adams sees me coming. "Child, am I glad you're here!" she calls out. "These chillun are 'bout to drive me crazy. I got no business takin' care of little ones at my age. I thought I could do it, but it's about got me down."

The relief I feel is indescribable. The weights holding me down drop away. I let out a huge sigh and begin breathing again when the twins race out from Mrs. Adams' living room.

"Where's Mama?" I ask.

"What? Not so much as a thank you!" she scolds. "I have these twins all afternoon and you don't even say 'Thank you.'"

"I'm so sorry, Mrs. Adams. I didn't mean to be rude, but I was so scared when they weren't home. I was sure Ms. Walker had taken them for good. I couldn't stand it if that happened." My words tumble out rapidly as I try to apologize, explain, and ask questions all at once.

"Thank you. Thank you for keeping them."

"It's all right, child. I was watching for the bus so you wouldn't be frightened, but the phone rang just as the bus arrived."

"Why are the twins here, Mrs. Adams? Where's Mama?"

"Child, how should I know? I doubt the good Lord Himself can tell where she is most of the time. All I know is Ms. Walker came by to see your mama. Right after she left, Glennie tole' me she was goin' to the store and asked would I watch the twins. That was noon and she's not back yet. I never knew it to take three hours to get groceries."

My heart takes another tumble. I know what Mrs. Adams doesn't know. Sometimes for Mama, "going to the store" doesn't mean the grocery. It means going for her fix. She could be gone for days.

It's a good thing Mama's not here. I feel like screaming and yelling and attacking her with both fists. Of course, I'd never hit Mama, but I'm so boiling mad I might say something I shouldn't. How can she tell me to be good and to do right when she can't even take care of her children for one day!

After feeding the twins, I put them at one end of the table with notebook paper and crayons. I make a row of A's on their papers. "Okay, guys, you make A's like this on your whole page and you'll be as smart as the kindergarten kids. When you get all finished, you can draw a picture on the back."

While they're busy writing their A's, I start my homework.

"Look at this Rosie. Did I do it right?"

"My A's are the best."

Do you like my A's?"

With all the interruptions, I can tell this is not a good arrangement, but my mind is made up. No matter what Mama does, my homework will be done tomorrow. I am determined to stay on honor roll.

The twins are in bed when Calvin comes home.

"Hey, Sis, got anything to eat?"

"You can check the fridge, but there's not much there."

As he wolfs down a peanut butter sandwich, I break the news. "Mama's gone again."

"Oh, man!" he groans. "Not already!"

"Mrs. Adams had the twins when I got home. She said Mama went to the store right after Ms. Walker left."

"This stinks!" Calvin mutters. "Those kids aren't our responsibility. They're Mama's."

"Do you want to be the one to tell her?" I demand. That shuts him up. No one tells Mama what her responsibility is.

Chapter 10

Lunch With The Teacher

"Excellent work!" I grin, reading the words written in green ink on my social studies report. Then I see, penciled in, the words "See me."

I wonder why Mrs. Bass wants to see me. It can't be about my work because I haven't missed a single assignment. Lakeshia and Tremayne have seen to that. Tremayne says our competition isn't fair if he gets more A's when I'm absent so much.

Maybe it's about my absences. There's nothing I can say about them. Not without getting Mama in trouble. I'll pretend I didn't see the note. Maybe she'll forget.

Uh-oh, here she comes. Thinking quickly, I raise my hand. "May I go to the restroom," I plead. "It's an emergency!"

She nods and I rush out.

Whew! I laugh at my reflection in the bathroom mirror. That worked well. In fact, I may have to try that little trick again. Almost as soon as the thought pops into my head, I drive it out. I can't spend my life in the school restroom just because I don't want Mrs. Bass to ask personal questions. Besides, if I do it again, she might think I'm sick and send me to the clinic. At some point, I'm going to have to face her and find out what she wants. It just won't be today.

It's easy to avoid her the next day because I'm home babysitting.

Mrs. Bass is ready for me when I return. "Deanna," she says, "every day I eat lunch with one of my students. Today, it's your turn."

I know she's telling the truth. Tremayne and Lakeshia have already eaten with her.

We're the last class to eat so I have five hours to dread lunch. What will we talk about? Can I keep the family secret about Mama being gone most of the time? More importantly, how will I save food to take home to Calvin and the twins?

At lunchtime, Mrs. Bass leads the way to a picnic table. I pick at my food wondering how to hide part of it to take home.

"Deanna," Mrs. Bass says, "I've been reviewing your goals. They're quite ambitious."

"Yes, Ma'am." I reply, wondering where this is going.

"I've looked at your records. You've been on honor roll since the first grade. Very impressive."

"Yes, Ma'am, I try. I want to stay on honor roll all the way through school," I answer proudly, looking straight at her. Maybe this lunch won't be so bad.

"You know, Deanna, when people are deciding who will get scholarships, grades are important, but they also look at other factors like dependability, participation in school activities, and attendance."

I know what's coming next and I want to plug my ears to keep from hearing it. My spirit sinks. The one person who gave me hope is taking it away.

Like I said before, Mrs. Bass doesn't play. She

46

comes right to the point. "So far this year, you've missed eight of the twenty school days."

"Yes, Ma'am." I'm not looking at her any more. Trying to hold in the anger rising up inside me, I stare at my plate and stir my food from side to side. It isn't fair. I can't help it if I'm not in school. They, whoever they are, ought to give some consideration for my doing well in spite of my absences. Of course, I don't say that to Mrs. Bass.

"Deanna, I hear by the grapevine that you're home babysitting. Is that correct?"

"I'll find a way to go to college," I say, totally ignoring her question.

"I'm sure you will," Mrs. Bass responds. "Is your mother ill?"

This woman! I wish she'd get off my case! "I'm here today, aren't I? Isn't that what's important? And who says I'm not dependable? Have I missed any assignments? Even one?" I snap at her.

"Whoa, whoa, Deanna! Calm down. I'm not your enemy. I'm trying to help."

"Sorry," I mumble.

"Look," she says, "I know you want to be in school. If you ever decide to tell me what's going on, I'll be here. I'm a good listener. Now, drink your milk and we'll go in. I've got some things to do before class."

"I'm going to save it for break time," I tell her, stuffing the still closed milk carton into my sweater pocket. Half my hot dog is already wrapped in a napkin in my other pocket.

"Well, be careful not to squish it. We don't want milk all over the classroom, do we?"

Hm, I think. She's okay for a white lady. If things get bad enough, maybe I'll explain about Mama.

Chapter 11

Ms. Walker Returns

Things are getting worse fast. When I get home, Calvin is not there, the twins are crying, and I've got a major cleaning job to do. Anthony didn't make it to the bathroom in time and both Sophie and Anthony are filthy from trying to clean up his mess. Yuk!

I put them in the shower and am in the middle of mopping the floor when I hear a knock at the door. I glance out and see Ms. Walker peering in the window.

Drat! I forgot to close the blinds. I duck back into the bathroom hoping she didn't see me. I close the bathroom door, shut off the shower water, and shush the twins. Quickly, I towel them dry.

The knocking continues, louder.

"I know you children are in there. I hear you moving around," Ms. Walker calls. "Open the door and let me in."

None of us budges.

I put my finger to my lips warning the twins to keep still.

The kitchen door creaks open. I hear footsteps crossing from the kitchen to the living room door. Who, I wonder, is that?

I crack the door open and peek out just as Mama opens the door.

"What do you want?" Mama asks sharply.

Ms. Walker stares at her dumbfounded before stammering, "I-I want to check on your children to make sure they're all right."

"Why wouldn't they be?" Mama demands.

Ms. Walker regains her composure. "Mrs. Brown, my office keeps getting reports that your children are being left home alone. Not only that, both Calvin and Deanna have been absent from school for at least eight days. You are required to have them in school. It's the law."

My thoughts are swirling. How does she know I've been absent? Who told her Mama was leaving us alone? How does Mama always seem to know when Ms. Walker is coming? This is her third visit and, somehow, Mama has managed to be here every time. My mind is so absorbed by questions that I am totally thrown by what happens next.

"Deanna Rose," Mama calls. "Get out here."

When Mama talks in that tone of voice, I move.

"Deanna, is Ms. Walker telling the truth? You been missin' school?"

I look down at the floor. What do I say? If I deny it, Ms. Walker will be able to prove I'm lying. If I admit it, there's no telling what Mama will do.

"Answer me!" Mama commands.

"Yes, Ma'am."

"Yes, Ma'am, what? Yes, you're going to answer me or yes, you've been missing school?"

"I've missed some school," I answer, "but I've kept up with my homework."

"Girl, when I send you out the door in the morning, I expect you to go to school. You understand me?"

"Yes, Ma'am."

Mama is so clever. She says the right words to satisfy Ms. Walker, but they have a different meaning. When she sends me out the door, I do go to school. The problem is she's hardly ever home to send me out the door.

"Now, Ms. Social Worker," Mama says indignantly, "please leave. I'm tired of your harassment!"

Ms. Walker looks from Mama to me and back again. I don't think she's satisfied with the situation, but what can she do? She's checked three times. Mama's been home every time and has reprimanded me in front of her.

Pulling herself up to her full height, which is still shorter than Mama, Ms. Walker answers icily, "I'm just doing my job. When I get a call, I am required to check. I will continue to do so." She turns and stalks away, her heels echoing her anger as she stomps down the sidewalk.

"Hmpf!" Mama snorts. "That lady don't know who she's messin' with."

I don't know what she means by that, but she must be a little concerned because she comes home after work the next few days.

Chapter 12

The Worst Christmas Ever

Christmas vacation is here. It's supposed to be a happy season, but all I feel is sadness and an empty ache inside for Mama's love. Last week was my twelfth birthday, but no one remembered it. Sometimes, I think that no one knows or cares about me and I want to scream to the world, "Look at me! I'm alive! I matter!"

I clearly don't matter to Mama who is gone most of the time. Life is harder because Calvin quit helping. For a while, he was mesmerized by AJ, but no more. Even she cannot persuade him to do his share. If it weren't for Papa Joe checking on us occasionally, I'd feel totally alone. At least, I won't have to worry about Sophie and Anthony during vacation. I'll be here to look after them.

I wonder if Papa Joe will dress up like Santa and put gifts under our tree like he did last year. Come to think of it, we don't have a tree yet and Christmas is only two days away.

"Mama," I ask, when she comes home from work, "when are we going to get our Christmas tree?"

"We're not," she replies brusquely.

"But Mama, it won't seem like Christmas without a tree."

"Christmas is just another day. You don't have a tree on other days. You don't need one now."

I can tell this is going to be an awful Christmas, but I don't know how awful it's going to be.

On Christmas morning, I'm awakened by laughter on the sidewalk in front of our home. "Hey, Keesh, watch this!" I recognize Tremayne's voice calling to Lakeshia. I crawl out of bed and peek out the window. Tremayne, Lakeshia, and Tyrell are laughing hilariously as they try to balance on their new roller blades. I wish I'd get some too, but that's not likely. Not wanting them to see me, I back away from the window.

Trying not to awaken Sophie, I tiptoe silently out to the kitchen. Mama's already there. "Merry Christmas, Mama," I say.

Startled, Mama turns away from me, but not before I see her removing the needle from her arm.

"Deanna Rose Blakely, you've got no business sneaking up on people like that," she yells, trying to cover the needle with a dishtowel.

"And you've got no business using drugs!" I shout back. Angry and hurt, I don't stop to think of the consequences.

Whang! Whap! Two quick slaps and I'm on the floor looking up at her.

"And you've got no business telling me my business!" she retorts, coming after me.

I try to back away, but she yanks me up. Shaking me, she snarls, "You didn't see nothin', you hear? Nothin'! You say you did and I'll say you're a liar. Understand?"

Numbly, I nod my head.

"Don't you shake your head at me!" Mama scolds. "I said, 'Do you understand?'"

53

"Yes, Ma'am," I answer sullenly, too scared to talk back again.

Christmas is supposed to be a day of love, but at that moment the hatred I feel toward Mama is indescribable.

I escape to my room so I won't have to share space with her.

Minutes later, she shoves Calvin and the twins ahead of her into my room. Striding to the window, she yanks the cord closing the venetian blinds.

"When I get home, these blinds better still be closed and you better still be here. No company either!"

I watch mutely as she slams the bedroom door. The clinking of the latch tells me that we're locked in.

Shortly after Mama leaves, there's a knock at the front door.

"Rosie, it's AJ. Open up."

The four of us sit in absolute silence afraid to answer even one of our best friends.

Next AJ raps on the window to my bedroom. "Deanna, you can come out. Your Mama's gone. Granny sent me to invite you to dinner."

No one answers. It's odd how Mama can control us even when she's not here.

The truth is I might have answered AJ, but the other three are so scared of Mama that they'd tell on me. I'm relieved when AJ finally goes home. All I need is for my friends to know we're locked in.

Calvin and I make up games to keep the twins occupied, but as the hours pass, we begin to get desperate. The twins haven't been to the bathroom and none of us has eaten. It won't do any good to climb out the window because we still can't get to the refrigerator or the bathroom. Mama locked the front door, too.

Around 2:30, there's another knock on the door. "Deanna Rose," Mrs. Adams calls. "Open the door. I brought you some Christmas dinner. It's nice and hot."

Calvin and I look at each other indecisively. I can't read his mind, but I'm thinking that we can't stay in here forever and starve. On the other hand, I will be utterly mortified if our friends see us crawling out the window.

Before we have time to decide, we hear Mrs. Adams again. "Oh, Joe, I'm so glad to see you. Lord knows what's happened to those little children. They could be lying in there dead. Rosie's doin' the best she can, but it just ain't right for Glennie to leave them like this. When I saw her goin' out in a huff early this morning, I sent AJ over to invite them to dinner, but AJ didn't hear a peep from them. I tell you it's not natural for four children to be that quiet. Those poor little tykes! You saw me trying to get them to open the door. I thought sure a turkey dinner would lure them out."

"Ruby Adams, please take a breath! One of these keys ought to work. We'll be in the house in a jiffy."

"I tell you, Joe, we've got to do something about them. Why, those little ones are wastin' away. They're bellies are getting' big and their arms and legs are spindly. Malnourished, that's what they are! Just the other day, I discovered Rosie and AJ are saving food from school to give those little ones. I never would have known it if I hadn't done the laundry and found part of a sandwich in AJ's pocket. She says Calvin's supposed to help too, but he's been skipping school. It's a crime.

That's what it is. I've called Ms. Walker, but somehow Glennie seems to know when she's coming and hightails it back here."

"Mrs. Adams," Papa Joe interrupts, "I know you're doing your best and I appreciate it. Right now, I need you to hush to see if we can hear them."

"I just pray to the good Lord that they're alive!"

"Ruby!" Papa Joe sounds exasperated.

"Rosie," he calls. "Come open the door."

"I can't," I yell, hoping he'll hear me. "We're locked in."

Finally, a key turns the lock.

"Well, I'll be!" Papa Joe exclaims. "No wonder they didn't come to the door. The bedroom door is locked from this side."

"Ooh, sweet Jesus," Mrs. Adams intones, "Don't let us find dead bodies on the other side of that door! Glennie's been actin' so crazy she coulda' killed them and locked the door behind her. If you hadn't had a key, we might never have found them."

"Ruby Adams, will you hush!" Papa Joe says firmly as he unlatches the door and pushes it open.

"Whoa, easy now!" Papa Joe steadies himself against the doorframe as all four of us try to squeeze through the door at once.

Mrs. Adams' hovers over us as we hungrily attack the first real meal we've had in months. "Tch, tch, tch. It's a shame, that's what it is," she mutters as she packs up the empty dishes and heads for home. "Poor little children."

Papa Joe goes to the porch and brings in presents: toys for each of the twins, and a basketball for

Calvin. He saves my gift until last. His eyes shine as he watches me open it.

"Papa Joe, it's beautiful," I exclaim, holding up an outfit that's almost like AJ's lace-up shirt with beads and sequins and her leather-laced slacks. A small diary falls from a pocket as I pick up the slacks.

"You're growin' up, Rosie," he says. "Thought you might like somethin' other than a toy."

"Thank you, thank you, thank you." I waltz to my room to try on my new outfit.

At that instant, Mama bursts through the door screaming, "What are you doing in my house? Get out! Get out this instant! Take this stuff with you! We don't need your charity!" Shouting like a crazy person, she throws the toys and the basketball out into the yard.

Thinking quickly, I stuff my outfit and diary under my bed, slip into the bathroom, and flush the toilet. Hearing that, she shrieks, "Deanna Rose, get out here. I told you not to let anyone in this house."

Papa Joe, frail as he is, stands between Mama and me. "Glennie," he says sternly, shaking his cane at her, "shut up and think. Rosie couldn't have let me in. You had them all locked in her room. I let myself in and I'm going to keep coming whenever I want. You don't deserve these children and they certainly don't deserve you."

The air is electric with hostility as the two of them glare angrily at each other. We four children look from Mama to Papa Joe wondering what will happen next. No one talks to Mama that way.

Papa Joe doesn't seem to know that. Staring straight into Mama's furious eyes, his voice cold and stern, he commands, "Glennie, go to your room. Stay there until you're sober. Go. Get out of my sight!"

Mama snarls, "You can't come into my home and order me around in front of my children!"

"I just did," he retorts icily. "Do what I tell you before I report you to the police for neglecting and abusing your children. Furthermore, those toys are coming back in and had better be here whenever I come."

I've never seen Mama take orders from anyone; but then, I've never seen Papa Joe so angry either. Mama stomps into her bedroom, slamming the door behind her.

I let out a huge sigh of relief and give Papa Joe a big hug.

Hugging me back, he says, "How about you come out to the porch and explain what Mrs. Adams meant about you and AJ bringing food home."

Sitting in the rocker I'd confiscated from the curb, I tell him about taking turns going to school, saving food for the twins, and AJ's help.

"Rosie, you are my Rise and Shine girl! I see what Mrs. Adams says about your doing your best. I'm so proud of you. If you ever feel you're in danger or if you need help, call me. I'll help if I can."

Chapter 13

Decisions

It's New Year's Day, a day of decisions for me. My goals are the same, but it's getting harder to stay on honor roll. Even with help from Tremayne and Lakeshia, I'm missing a lot of class work and discussions. I do my homework, but I don't understand it like I would if I were in school every day. One thing is clear. I'll never be able to go to college if I can't get out of the house to go to school. I love Sophie and Anthony and I wouldn't hurt them for the world, but I'm not their mother. Besides if I don't go to school, they'll be without food .

Mama's at work and I'm busy revising my childcare plan. I've learned not to count on Calvin. I have to figure a way to take care of the twins and still go to school.

Pulling a sheet of paper from my notebook, I jot down some notes.

When Mama isn't home, I'll dress the twins before I leave, give them something to play with, give them food if we have any, and lock them in my room so they can't get into Mama's drugs. I'll ask Papa Joe to get a key for AJ so she can look in on them before she goes to school. Maybe Papa Joe can check on them sometimes too. I know it's not safe to leave them alone, but I don't know what else to do. Besides, didn't Mama tell me in front of Ms. Walker that I better not miss any more school?

While Sophie and Anthony are taking a nap, I slip quietly out the door and run across the street to AJ's house. Mrs. Adams greets me. "Everything okay, Deanna?"

"Yes, Ma'am. Is AJ home?"

"She's in her room working on her science project. Where are the little ones? You didn't leave them alone, did you?"

"They're asleep. I came to see if AJ could come over."

"Goodness gracious, Deanna, you shouldn't leave them alone for even one moment. Of course, you're a child yourself. I can't expect you to know that. Too much responsibility is what you've got. Go on, child. It's all right with me if she wants to go with you."

Back in our duplex, I share my plans with AJ.

She is a little skeptical. "I don't know, Rosie, if this'll work or not. How will I know if your mama's home? I don't want to walk in while she's there."

After a moment's thought, I say, "We're not allowed to have the shades open when Mama's gone. If she's here, I'll raise the one by the front door just a few inches."

"What if Granny catches me? She's bound to see me, especially if I come over every day. She'd report your mama for sure if she knew I was checking on the twins. She doesn't want me anywhere near here unless you're home. She says bad things are happening here."

"Would she see you if you came to the back door? I could have Papa Joe give you that key."

"I don't know. Sometimes, she watches until I get out of sight. What I can do is leave a little earlier and double back. That'll work unless one of the neighbors sees me and tells her."

I give her a hug. "Thanks, AJ, you're a real friend! I know it's not a great plan, but I just have to go to school."

"Let's hope it works."

"I'll call Papa Joe to see if he'll help."

"He will, I'm sure. He always says that nothing is too good for his Rise and Shine Rosie. He's really proud of you. He says that no matter how bad things get, you always look for a way to make them better."

When she leaves, I call Papa Joe.

"What's up, Rosie? Is something wrong?"

"Nothing's wrong, Papa Joe. I called to find out your work schedule."

"Most of the time, it's from nine to six. Why do you ask?"

"Do you get any time off for lunch?"

"Yes, I'm usually off from 11:30 – 12:30, but you still haven't told me why you want to know."

"Papa Joe, do you think you could swing by to check on the twins during lunch? I'm trying to figure out a way to go to school so I can stay on honor roll and get a college scholarship."

"Rosie, you're an amazing young lady. Tell you what. You let me know when your mama's not home and I'll plan to spend my lunchtime with them those days. Mind you now, I can't do it every day, but I'll do it as often as I can."

"Ooh, Papa Joe, I love you! You're my guardian

angel!"

"Well, nothing's too good for my Rise and Shine Rosie."

"One more thing, Papa Joe, can you get a key made to the kitchen door so I can give it to AJ. She's going to help, too."

"You're really quite a planner," he chuckled.

With that plan in place, I tackle the next problem. What am I going to do about Mama? I'm only twelve, but I know this plan won't work forever. I want Mama to get off drugs and be home with us again. I want the old Mama back, the one who did homework with me and encouraged me to do my best, the one who had dreams of a better life.

I know I can't go on for six more years like this. I don't want to hate my own mother, but she's hard to like when she's on drugs. If I could get her help without getting her in trouble, I'd report her, but I'm afraid the social worker would take Sophie and Anthony. I couldn't bear to lose them. I'll wait. If the plan works, I can last until summer.

Chapter 14

Disaster

It's February. So far, my plan has worked well. Papa Joe and AJ are doing their part and I'm keeping up with my schoolwork. Surprisingly, Mama's been home one or two days a week. On those days, AJ and Papa Joe stay away.

Today, the plan comes to a screeching halt.

I do as much of my homework on the bus as possible so I can give my full attention to the twins when I'm home. I'm so engrossed in my pre-algebra problems I don't hear the sirens or notice the bus driver pulling over to let an ambulance pass.

"Rosie! Rosie!" Tremayne shouts, "that ambulance stopped at your house!"

As the bus rolls to my stop, I elbow my way to the front. As soon as the door opens, I race to the ambulance, shrieking, "What's wrong? Who's hurt?"

Anthony, his leg sticking out at an odd angle, is being lifted onto a gurney.

"No!" I scream, "No!"

Mama is running toward us, screeching at the top of her lungs, "My baby! Not my baby!"

Sophie, who has blood all over her clothes, lets out a loud wail as she tries to escape Mrs. Adams' clutch.

Kids from the bus crowd around the medical technicians.

"Back off! Give us room!" a medic barks as they lift the gurney into the ambulance.

Climbing in beside Anthony, Mama turns to shout at me, "You watch Sophie! I'll see about you later!"

Her shrill angry tone tells me that's a threat.

When the ambulance pulls away, I go to comfort Sophie. She clings to my neck when I pick her up. "What happened?" I ask, wondering how they got out of my bedroom. "Can you tell me?"

Between sobs, she stammers, "H-he falled down!"

"Can you show me where?"

Still sobbing, she shakes her head up and down.

Mrs. Adams comes with us, muttering all the way, "I knew this would come to no good. You poor children, being left alone all the time! I shouldn't talk about your mama, but she oughta' be whipped. She's got no business havin' children! Poor, poor, little tykes! I never ran so fast in all my life when I heard those ear-piercing screams. Good thing I was out in the yard. That child could have died!"

The kitchen wall and floor are spattered with blood and blood-soaked towels are on the table. A chair is lying on its side.

"Sophie, tell me what happened."

"Anthony climbed up there to get some food and he falled down," she said, pointing to the top cupboard shelf.

"Sophie, we don't have any food up there," I say, peeling off her bloody clothes."

"Uh-huh, I seed Mama put it there."

Oh, no! What she saw Mama put there was

drugs.

I'm so worried about Anthony, I don't even see Tremayne standing there until he says, "Here are your books from the bus. Where do you want me to put them?"

"Thanks, Tremayne. I didn't know I left them. Just put them on the couch."

"Looks like you need some help. Got a sponge?"

"You don't have to do that," I protest, but he's insistent. I wish Calvin were that helpful.

I clean Sophie and put her down for a nap while Tremayne helps Mrs. Adams clean the kitchen.

Mrs. Adams gathers up all the bloody towels and clothes. "Deanna," she says, "I'll take these home and wash them. If Glennie's not home by supper time, you and Sophie come over for a bite to eat." Turning to Tremayne, she says, "You, young man, better get on home. I don't expect Deanna's mama will want you here when she gets back."

"I'm leaving in a minute, Mrs. Adams."

"No, you're leaving now," she orders. "You're not staying here with Deanna."

"You gonna be okay?" he asks.

"Yeah, I'll be fine."

"If you're not in school tomorrow, I'll bring your assignments." Then quietly he whispers, "Don't worry. I won't tell anyone they were home by themselves."

After he leaves, I get crayons and paper for Sophie so she can draw while I try to finish my homework. My mind and my thoughts feel like two separate parts of my head battling each other. My mind says I need to focus on my math while my thoughts keep flitting back to Anthony's screams, the blood, and Mama's threat. I don't blame her for being upset about Anthony, but his being injured is not my fault. She should be upset with herself for not being a better mother.

Of course, I have to admit that if I had been home, Anthony wouldn't be in the hospital now. I know I latched the bedroom door when I left this morning. Either AJ or Papa Joe must have left the bedroom door unlocked when they came to check on the twins.

One thing I can't figure out is how Mama knows when to come home. Where was she when she realized the ambulance was at our house?

Mama and Anthony still are not home when I finish my homework. I wonder what's taking so long. I hope and pray Anthony didn't take any of the drugs. If he did and the doctors discover it, he could be taken away from Mama. If that happens, Sophie and I could be next.

I know what I have to do and I'm ready to do it. I have to report Mama. She can't get help unless someone who knows the facts reports her. That someone is me.

Chapter 15

Time to Tell

I lie awake all night thinking about what to say. Needing all the confidence I can muster, I put on my best outfit – the one Papa Joe gave me for Christmas. Wearing it makes me feel like he's close beside me.

I try to act as if this is an ordinary day, but believe me, there's nothing ordinary about reporting your own mother for drug abuse. All morning, my mind keeps flipping back and forth between the math lesson and what I plan to say.

Mrs. Bass goes from desk to desk checking our math work. When she gets to mine, I slide a paper out from my book just far enough for her to see it. In tiny letters, I've written, "I need to talk to you in private."

She folds it and slips it in her pocket. Right before physical education class, she whispers, "Stay here. I'll ask Coach to excuse you today."

By the time she returns, my stomach is doing loop-de-loops. My mouth feels like it's stuffed with cotton and no matter how much I lick my lips, they feel dry and cracked. Oddly, my palms are sweaty and clammy. I trust Mrs. Bass, but what I'm about to do might change my whole life.

"What did you need to see me about, Deanna?"
"My mother."
"Is she still ill?"

"Yes, but not like you think. She needs help, but if I tell the kind of help she needs, I might lose my brothers and sister."

"Whoa, this sounds serious! What's wrong with her?"

"She uses drugs."

"Is that why you miss so much school?"

"Yes, Ma'am."

"Deanna, we need to include the principal in this conversation. She knows the right people to contact for help. Would you like me to go with you?"

Numbly, I nod my head yes, and follow Mrs. Bass.

I've never been to Ms. Richmond's office and I'm afraid of what she'll do when I tell her my problem. All the way there, I talk to myself. Take a deep breath, Deanna. Stay calm. You're trying to help Mama. You're doing the right thing. Even with all my self-talk, I'm nervous and jittery.

Ms. Richmond looks up from her paperwork when Mrs. Bass raps on the doorframe.

"I know you're busy," Mrs. Bass says, "but we need a few minutes of your time."

"Is Deanna in trouble?"

"No, no. She needs our help. I'll let her tell you about it."

I can feel the th-thump, th-thump of my heart. It's pounding so hard my ears hurt. I sit on my hands to keep them from shaking. Taking a deep breath, I plunge into my prepared speech.

"I need help with my mother. I don't want her arrested because we need her at home, but she's a drug addict and a dealer. Are there any programs that help people get off drugs without getting them in trouble?"

"Yes, there are," Ms. Richmond answers, "but for any program to be successful, a person has to want to stop."

"I'm the one who wants her to stop, but maybe she'll want to if the police scare her by telling her they suspect she's dealing drugs. She has to stop because it's dangerous for my little brother and sister. Just yesterday, Anthony fell off the counter and broke his leg trying to get food he saw Mama put in the cupboard. It wasn't food. It was drugs."

"How do you know it was drugs?" Ms. Richmond asked.

"One night after Mama locked me in my room, I heard whispering in the kitchen. I peeked through a crack in the door and saw her give a white man little bags of powder. Then he gave her money. After he left, I watched her take something from her pocket and put it on the top cupboard shelf. The next day, when she was gone, I climbed up and looked. It's the same kind of stuff the police officer showed us during Red Ribbon Week. I also saw her shooting up on Christmas morning."

"Is your mother being on drugs the reason you miss so much school?"

This is the tricky part. Instead of telling about Mama being gone so often, I answer, "Sometimes she doesn't feel well so I stay home to help."

Ms. Richmond pauses to think. Finally, she asks, "If I can get her into a drug treatment center, do you have relatives who can take care of you children while she's away?"

"I have some aunts, Papa Joe, and our neighbor, Mrs. Adams. We'll stay anywhere just so we're not separated."

"I'm required to call social services with this information. A caseworker will talk with you and then with your mother."

"No! I don't want to talk with anyone else. You can tell the caseworker what I told you. Say you heard it somewhere, but don't tell anyone you heard it from me! I don't want Mama to know I told!"

"Deanna, you'll be fine. I'll stay with you if you'd like. Don't worry about your mother discovering that you told. That's confidential information and the case worker isn't allowed to share it without your permission."

I leave her office feeling more light-hearted than I have in a long time. When Mama's off drugs and back home, things will be the way they used to be. I soon learn how wrong I am.

On the way to class after lunch, I see Ms. Richmond coming toward us. She glances at me, then speaks to Mrs. Bass who nods and says, "Give me a few minutes."

In class, Mrs. Bass says, "Deanna, please take this note to the office for me." On it, she writes, "The social worker is here." She knows how to keep private things private.

My spirits fall when I see Ms. Walker in the office. She's already tried three times to catch Mama being gone. Every time, Mama has appeared. There's no way she'll be able to help.

"Your principal says you need some assistance, Deanna."

"No, Ms. Walker," I respond politely. "My mama is the one who needs assistance. I don't mean any disrespect, but are you sure you can help her? You've been to the house three times already. She says what you want to hear and you leave."

"That's not exactly true. Twice, she was home. The third time, I was checking on your attendance. I heard her tell you when she sends you out the door, she expects you to go to school. You admitted that you had been skipping."

"See," I say defiantly, all pretense of politeness gone, "you proved my point. You heard what you wanted to hear. I didn't say I skipped school. I said I missed school. Ms. Richmond can show you my grades. A person who wants to skip school doesn't stay on honor roll."

"Skipped? Missed? What's the difference?"

"Ms. Walker, I didn't come to talk about me. I came to get help for Mama."

Turning to Ms. Richmond, I ask, "May I go back to class?"

Ms. Richmond raises her eyebrows in surprise. "No, Deanna. This is your opportunity to get help. You need to finish what you came to do."

Directing her attention to Ms. Walker, she says, "I think it would be helpful if you listen to Deanna's story."

Hearing that, Ms. Walker has little choice. She pushes her tiny round glasses up on her pudgy nose, turns to face me, and says, "I'm listening."

I tell my story again just as I told it this morning. I omit the parts about being left alone, taking food home from school, and my plan for taking care of the twins. I finish by emphasizing, "Ms. Walker, I want Mama to get help without knowing I'm the one who told and I don't want to be separated from Calvin and the twins. Can you do those things?"

Ms. Walker looks at me with more respect than before. "I definitely will not tell your mother who reported her. If we didn't keep that information confidential, no one would report anyone. If she agrees to get help, I'll do my best to keep the four of you together, but I can't make any promises."

"At least, keep the twins and me together. They need me."

The last hour of the day seems like ten. I dread facing Mama. She'll be in a horrid mood if Ms. Walker has already been there. My head aches. I feel like a heavy fist is hammering at my heart.

The bus ride is way too short. I walk into the house not knowing what to expect.

Everything seems normal. Anthony, his leg in a cast, is playing on the floor. Sophie, who is chattering away beside him, jumps up for her daily afternoon hug. I don't see Mama, but the blinds are open so she must be here.

The normal world disappears when I go to my room to change clothes. The blinds are drawn and the room is dark. I reach for the light switch and gasp as Mama pins me to the wall, her switchblade knife against my throat.

Chapter 16

Confrontation

I try to scream, but no sound comes out. I feel like I'm going to throw up. My legs give way like soft rubber as I sink slowly to the floor. Everything around me seems hazy and blurry. The only clear thought is she's going to kill me!

With the switchblade held sideways in her fist, Mama kneels over me, grabs my shoulders, and starts shaking me. Each shake is punctuated with another word. Through the fogginess, I hear, "If-I-find-out-you-reported-me, – it's-the-last-thing-you'll-ever-do! You-hear-me?"

Before I can answer, Sophie opens the door. "Rosie, will you please tie my shoes?"

"Stay out!" Mama screams, jumping to her feet and stuffing the switchblade into her pocket.

"Mama, why are you and Rosie in the dark?"

"Go away!" She shoves Sophie into the hall, slams the door shut, and turns toward me.

From somewhere deep inside, anger and the will to survive overcome my fears. I jump up, yank open the blinds, and face Mama, realizing for the first time that I'm as tall as she is. We stand there glaring, fear and hatred flashing wordlessly between us.

Finally, Mama breaks the silence, her words slicing through the icy atmosphere.

"I'm your Mama. How dare you report me for using drugs!"

Filled with anger, I retort, "Y-you tried to kill me!"

"Girl, if I'd been trying, you'd be dead! Answer my question. Why did you report me?"

"What makes you think I did?" I snap, refusing to back down.

"Think? I don't think! I know! Ms. Walker just left. She said someone called her about my being on drugs. You're the only one who knew. Because of you, I have to go for a drug test Thursday morning."

I turn Mama's misleading-without-lying tactic back on her.

"Well, I didn't call her. I was in school all day and I never once asked to use the phone. If you don't believe me, call and ask." I know talking to her this way is dangerous, but I'm so upset, I can't stop myself. "Maybe someone from the hospital called because you were acting so weird when Anthony broke his leg. Maybe Ms. Walker has gotten so many calls about you, she suspects you're on drugs. Maybe the medics reported you! They heard you threaten me."

Mama's eyes narrow to slit size as she snarls through clenched teeth, "Your life won't be worth living if I find out it was you. And I'll tell you something else," she adds belligerently. "Ain't nobody gonna find no drugs in me."

* * * * *

All night, I toss and turn, trying to think of what else to do. I can't run away and leave Sophie and Anthony alone. I have to come up with something soon or Mama may really kill me.

I'm not the only one awake. The familiar sound of Mama's dry, scratchy cough penetrates the paper-thin walls. Several times during the night, she gets up for water. It doesn't seem to help. I used to feel safe when I heard her cough because I knew she was home. After she pulled that knife today, I'll never feel safe again.

Papa Joe always says God loves us all. The way Mama's treating us, I don't understand how God can love her. I sure don't feel loved right now, but I try talking to God anyway. I know He doesn't like what I'm saying and, to tell the truth, I feel guilty about it. You're never supposed to ask for bad things to happen to people, but the only way I think things will get better for us is if Mama dies. It may be wrong, but that's what I pray for.

I wish with all my heart Papa Joe would come live with us or that he'd let us live with him, but he already said he couldn't keep us. In my mind, I keep hearing him say, "My Rise and Shine Rosie, I'm proud of you. You'll do all right." If he knew about Mama's switchblade, he might not think that.

Chapter 17

More Decisions and Dead Ends

I'm in the middle of our Monday morning math test when the intercom blares. "Mrs. Bass, please send Deanna Rose Blakely to the office."

My classmates' questioning stares seem to bore holes through me as I give Mrs. Bass my test.

"You can finish it later," she assures me, giving my shoulder a friendly squeeze.

I'm surprised to see Ms. Walker in Ms. Richmond's office.

"Deanna, I got your mother's drug tests results back. They showed no drugs in her system."

How can that be? I know what I've seen. I know she uses and sells.

Suddenly Mama's actions make sense.

"Ms. Walker, she drank tons of water after you told her she'd have to be tested. She told me you wouldn't find any drugs in her. Please, test her again, only don't tell her ahead of time. Please, she needs help!"

I don't say that we all need help, that Sophie and Anthony are almost always alone, that Mama pulled a knife on me, or that we have hardly any food at home. All those thoughts are tumbling around in my head, but somehow I think if Mama is better, everything else will improve. Maybe, if she gets help kicking her habits, she'll see the harm she's doing. Maybe she'll go back to being the Mama I used to love.

My thoughts are interrupted by Ms. Walker's parting words, "Well, Deanna, there's really nothing more I can do. She passed the drug test. I've got no reason to go back. If I do, she'll think I'm harassing her."

I return to class. I try to pay attention, but in the back of my mind, I wonder how I can make Ms. Walker believe me.

The needles, I decide. That's it! I'll bring in the needles!

Early the next morning, I peek into Mama's room. She's coughing, but asleep. Tiptoeing away from her door, I move a chair to the kitchen counter, climb up, and quietly open the cupboard door. A cockroach runs across my fingers as I reach for the needles. Startled, I gasp and jerk away, knocking the chair back against the stove with a loud clang. I freeze in place, praying that Mama won't wake up.

"W-Who's out there? What's happening?" she calls out, her words thick and slurred.

"It's just me, Mama. I tripped over a chair. Go back to sleep." Quickly, I grab two needles, jump down, wrap them in a paper towel, and stuff them in a paper bag. I hide them in the bottom of my backpack where no one can find them by accident. If I'm caught with them before I get to the office, I know I'll be suspended from school. I have to take the risk. We need help.

At school, I gulp down my orange juice. Usually, I love cinnamon toast, but today, it feels like a lump of cardboard in my throat. I slip the box of cereal into my pocket for the twins and ask to be excused from the cafeteria. We're supposed to wait until the bell rings, but I have to get to class ahead of the others.

Mrs. Bass looks up from her work. "Good morning, Deanna, shouldn't you be in the cafeteria?"

"Yes, Ma'am, but I need to see Ms. Richmond. Will you please write me a pass?"

"I will, but it's almost time for the bell. Ms. Richmond may not see you during DEAR time." DEAR means Drop Everything and Read. Everyone in our school has to read for fifteen minutes the first thing every morning.

"I know, but this is really, really important."

"Well, all right, but don't be surprised if you get sent back."

Clutching my backpack, I hurry to the office. I'm almost there when the bell rings. Mrs. Richmond, a book in her hand, is just closing her door.

"Mrs. Richmond," I call out. "Mrs. Richmond may I talk to you? Please?"

She looks at her book, then at the clock, then back at me. I hope that she'll say yes.

She doesn't disappoint me. "Deanna, I know it must be important or you wouldn't be here during DEAR time. Come in. What do you need? Is it about your mother again?"

Without speaking, I dig into my backpack and pull out the paper bag. Carefully, I unwrap the needles and dump them on her desk.

"Ms. Richmond, I know Ms. Walker doesn't believe me, but these are Mama's needles. I took them from the cupboard this morning. Are these enough proof?"

Ms. Richmond raises an eyebrow, purses her lips, and peers at me over her glasses. "Deanna, I'm going to call Ms. Walker and the police. I don't know what either of them will say or do. They might end up taking all of you away from your mother. Are you prepared for that?"

"Only if we can stay together. The twins need me. I'm the only one who cares about them. It'd be terrible if we were separated. Maybe someone would take us in long enough for Mama to get help."

"You go back to class. I'll make those calls and we'll see what happens."

I start to leave, but remembering how embarrassed and conspicuous I felt when my classmates stared at me yesterday, I turn back for one more favor. "Mrs. Richmond, if anyone comes, is there a way you can get me to the office without calling on the intercom? I don't want the other kids to know about this. They might talk and Mama would find out I'm the one who told."

She writes a note and hands it to me. Give this to Mrs. Bass, Deanna. I think this will take care of the situation."

Back in class, I try to concentrate. For brief moments, snatches of information about science project procedures stick to my spinning mind. For longer periods, I wonder what will happen to us when Mama goes for treatment and what life will be like when she's back home. Will she be like the Mama I remember?

My thoughts are interrupted by the blaring intercom.

"Mrs. Bass, would you please send someone dependable to the office to help me?"

About half the hands go up and the kids start calling out, "Pick me! Pick me!"

79

"Quiet! I'm going to pick someone who is not waving her hands and shouting out."

My hand is down because I don't want to go. I can't afford to miss out on the directions. Mrs. Bass pauses, looking around the room. "Deanna, would you go please?"

A police officer is waiting in Ms. Richmond's office. I've got to hand it to Ms. Richmond. That was a pretty clever way of getting me here.

"Deanna, tell Officer Ryan about these needles."

When I finish, Officer Ryan shakes his head like he can't believe what he's hearing. "Give me your address. We'll get right on it."

Yes! Finally, something is going to be done! Hope surges through me. The fear that's smothered me since I first saw Mama selling drugs starts melting away.

"I live in the Golden Oaks projects, Apartment 141."

His face clouds over. "You live where? In Golden Oaks?"

"Yes, Sir."

"Ma'am," he addresses Ms. Richmond. "Golden Oaks is in the Kenley Park jurisdiction. It's outta my territory. I'm really sorry, but I can't help you."

My shoulders sag as waves of disappointment engulf me. My face scrunches up as I struggle to keep from crying.

Seeing my despair, Officer Ryan picks up the phone. "Let me call Sergeant Tolley in Kenley Park. He's a friend of mine who works drug cases. He'll help if he can."

Luckily, Sergeant Tolley's shift is just starting and

he's able to come right away.

I repeat my story. He lets out a long, whistling sigh. "Sounds like you've been in trouble for some time," he says.

"No, Sir," I answer politely. "It's my mother who's in trouble. She needs help."

"You say there are other needles there?"

"Yes, Sir, I brought only two. If I had brought more, she would have noticed."

"I can go in with a search warrant, but I'll need probable cause. To get one, I'll have to use your name, Deanna."

"No! No! You can't do that! If Mama knows I told, she'd kill me. I don't mean she'd really kill me, but she'd be very angry and there's no telling what she'd do." The truth is she might kill me, but I can't let him know that.

"Is there anyone else I could talk to who knows what your mother is doing?"

"The only ones who know for sure are her customers and suppliers. I think the neighbors suspect, but do they know? I don't think so."

"Well, little lady, the best I can do without using your name is to put surveillance on your house, but I can't guarantee that we'll catch her. We don't have the manpower to have someone there full time. Meanwhile, I'll take the needles with me. Bringing them was a very brave thing to do, but we don't want you getting caught with them, do we? I'm sorry I can't help more."

When he leaves, I sit staring at the carpet patterns. I can't keep going up and down this roller coaster of hope and despair. Maybe I should have let him use my name.

Ms. Richmond sits there quietly, letting me think. Finally, she says, "I'm sorry, Deanna. I thought the police would be able to help. I'll talk to the guidance counselor. She might have access to other agencies that could help. I'm also going to give you my phone number. If you ever need to talk, call me."

"Thank you," I whisper, getting up to leave. I'm grateful that she cares, but I doubt that she'll be able to do more than she's already done.

At that moment, Ms. Walker is ushered into the office.

"Oh, it's you again, Deanna. What's happening now?" She addresses me as if I were a nuisance – a pesky gnat that won't go away.

Ms. Richmond answers for me. "Deanna brought in some needles to prove her mother is using drugs. She says there are more at home. We've already called the police, but they need probable cause before they can search. They've said they'll watch the house when they have people available."

Ms. Walker looks at me, shaking her head. "Deanna, there's nothing more I can do except to keep checking whenever I get a call. Your mama's always there when I come and her drug tests come back negative."

All the anger and hurt and fear I have held inside start churning to the surface. Most of the time, I stay calm when talking to adults because I know getting upset won't help, but today, I've had too many ups and downs. I know I'm going to say something I shouldn't, but no amount of trying will keep it in. I turn on Mrs. Walker.

"Ms. Walker, the only time my mother is home is

when she's drunk or bombed out. Somehow she knows when you're coming. Maybe someone in your office warns her when you're on the way. All I know is I'm a child. Before my mother started on drugs, she taught me that my job is to learn. You're an adult. Your job is to help my mother. I know how to do my job. You don't seem to know how to do yours!" I snatch up my backpack and storm out of the office.

Chapter 18

Homeless

"Hey, you!" Tremayne elbows me in the ribs as he squeezes between Lakeshia and me on the bus. "Is everything okay? You looked upset when you came back to class today. Are you all right?

"Everything's fine."

"You sure? All day, you've been acting like you lost your best friend."

"I said I'm fine!" My answer is sharper than it needs to be, but I really don't want to talk to anyone right now.

"Sure, whatever."

I can tell he doesn't believe me.

When the bus reaches my stop, I know instantly something is wrong. The maintenance truck Papa Joe drives is parked at the curb. He's at the door of the bus before I get there. Flames of fear race through my mind as he puts his grimy, work-soiled arm around my shoulders and wordlessly heads to Mrs. Adams' porch.

"What's wrong, Papa Joe? Are the twins all right? Did they get hurt again? Why are you here?" With each unanswered question, my voice rises in alarm.

He grips my trembling hand in his strong firm one and motions for me to sit.

"Rosie, the twins are fine, but your mama is too stirred up for you to go home. Mrs. Adams called me because Glennie's been yelling and slamming things around all afternoon. The police have driven by several times today. She thinks you called them on her. Says you stole something from her. Says you ain't never gonna' live in the same house with her again. Tried to tell me you was usin' drugs because she found needles on the top shelf when she was cleaning. I told her I knew better. Not my Rise and Shine Rosie. She says you can go rise and shine somewhere else. I think she'll calm down after a bit, but I want you to stay away for a few days."

A loud keening wail rises from deep within me. I beat Papa Joe's chest with my fists. "It's not fair!" I scream. "She's the one using drugs! She leaves us alone all the time without food. I have to miss school to take care of the twins while she's out shooting up! She even pulled a knife on me, Papa Joe! It's not fair!" Papa Joe wraps his arms around me and pins mine tight so I can't hit him anymore and lets me cry.

When I finally cry myself out, I tell him, "Papa Joe, I don't feel like rising and shining anymore. It's too hard."

"Rosie, you don't have a choice. You've got the same gift inside you Grandma Rose had. No matter how bad things get, it's your nature to find a way out. Sometimes clouds cover the sky, but behind them the sun is waiting. Know what would happen if the sun decided not to shine? After a while, it wouldn't be able to hold itself in. It would shine anyway. That's your gift, Rosie."

He gives me time to think about that.

After a long silence, I say, "Papa Joe, Mama's right.

85

I did steal two of her needles. I took them to school and reported her. She was so stoned I didn't think she'd notice. I was trying to get someone to help her, but everybody has a reason why they can't."

"I don't know that anyone can help your mama. She thinks she's okay as long as no one catches her. What you did was very brave, but in her mind, you've brought danger to her. I talked to your Aunt Dottie. You'll be staying with her for a while."

"But what about the twins? They can't stay by themselves at night. Half the time, Mama's either drunk or high. I have to be here for them."

Mrs. Adams, who has been hovering just inside the door with her nosy self, steps out onto the porch. "Now don't you go worrying about those little tykes. Do you think I don't know you've had AJ and your Papa Joe checking on them? I've been keeping an eye on them myself and so has Mrs. Morris."

"Mrs. Morris! Tremayne's mom? You mean Tremayne knows what's going on?

Oh, no! How can I face him again? He'll hate me if he thinks Mama is on drugs!"

"Child, listen to yourself. That boy doesn't hate you. Hasn't he brought you all your assignments when you've missed school? Would he do that if he hated you? Have you heard a word about yourself in school? His lips have been buttoned down so tight it would take a crowbar to pry them open. Oh, I'd say he likes you all right. You're blind as a bat if you don't know that. Anyway, I've been peeking in on those poor little tykes every chance I get. It's been about to worry me to death. Mrs. Morris and I have been keeping after Ms. Walker, too. She knows what's going on, but she can't prove it. You're not alone, child."

For once, I'm glad she's nosy.

Chapter 19

Death of an Angel

My stay at Aunt Dot's lasts only a few weeks. I would stay longer because she's my favorite aunt, but her boyfriend, Jermaine, is way too friendly with me. When he thinks no one is looking, he brushes up against me and touches me where he shouldn't. I always try to be near other people when he's around, but even then, I have to watch him. Aunt Dot is not stupid. I hear her at night reaming him out when she thinks I'm asleep. Jermaine just laughs at her. He says it sure feels good to have his woman jealous. I'm not surprised when Papa Joe comes to get me.

Papa Joe's skin sags on him and he leans more heavily on his cane. I don't like to see him looking this old and frail. He's always been so strong.

"Rosie girl, I think your mama has settled down enough for you to go home. She says she feels real bad about that knife thing. Says she was out of her head with Ms. Walker pestering her so much. Gave me the knife so you won't have to worry about it."

Papa Joe leaves off the beginning of his sentences. I used to try to copy him, but Mama wouldn't hear of it. Funny. She wants me to use book talk, but look how she acts.

"Says she wants you back home again. Now that it's summer, she won't have to worry about the twins during the day."

"Hunh, all she worries about is herself and where her next fix is coming from."

"I should have said I won't have to worry about them. When you're there, I know they're safe."

"Papa Joe, why can't you live with us? The only time I feel safe is when you're there. Mama listens to you when she won't listen to anyone else."

His face clouds over. "Baby doll, I just can't. Someday, you'll understand. Listen, if you ever need help and I'm not here, go straight to Mrs. Adams. She's nosy, but it's a good nosy. She looks out for you when Glennie's not home. I gave her some phone numbers for you to call if you ever need anything.

I have a bad feeling about this conversation.

"Papa Joe, where are you going? You can't leave! You can't! I need you!"

"Rosie, as long as I'm around here on this earth, I won't leave you."

For the next two weeks, life is fairly normal. Not normal like it is for other kids, but normal meaning Mama's not threatening to kill me when she's home which isn't often.

Sometimes, when she's gone at night, Calvin and I sleep on the floor by the door so we'll know if anyone tries to break in. Tonight is one of those nights. A little after 4:00 a.m., I dream that a white light is shining through the window. It looks like an angel raising its hand. It looks at me for a few seconds then fades from view.

"Sis," Calvin whispers, poking me, "I just dreamed I saw an angel at the window."

I'm wide awake now. "Me too. I had the same dream. What do you think it means?"

"Dunno. Maybe it was Mrs. Adams checking on us or lights from a patrol car."

"I don't think so, Calvin. It wasn't that kind of light. Police cars and flashlights don't look like angels."

I can't get back to sleep. What did the dream mean? Since Calvin and I both saw it, maybe it wasn't a dream. Maybe it was a real angel. Why would it come here?

I'm up and dressed when I hear Mrs. Adams's phone ring. I've never heard it before, but it's loud and clear today. I guess it's too early for traffic and people noises to drown it out.

Mrs. Adams' shrieking, "What! Oh, no! Oh, dear Jesus! Those poor, poor children!" is forever etched in my memory.

The phone call has to be about us. We're the only ones I know whom she calls those poor, poor children. My world crashes around me as I eavesdrop.

"Oh, Lord! What more can happen to those dear little children? What will they do without him? Yes, yes, I'll tell Deanna. I don't know how, but it's my duty since their mama's not home. Oh, my, my, my! I didn't expect this! What will happen now? Glennie actin' the fool and Joe gone! Why, Deanna Rose is barely holding things together as it is! I don't know how she'll manage without her guardian angel. That's what she calls him. He has been too. He's looked out after her even when she didn't know it."

Fear I've never known before, not even when Mama tried to kill me, sweeps over me in great waves.

On legs that feel like lead weights, I race across the street, screaming, "Mrs. Adams, Mrs. Adams, what's wrong with Papa Joe? Where is he? He told me he'd never leave! He promised!"

I fling myself into Mrs. Adams' outstretched arms and bury my face in her shoulder. Wrapping her wrinkled old arms around me, she hugs me tight. "There, there, darlin'," she comforts me. "Your Papa Joe's gone all right, but he didn't leave you of his own will. Died early this morning, he did. When the angels come after you, you have to go."

Startled, I pull away. I can't believe what I'm hearing. How did Mrs. Adams know about the angel? "Angels! Wh-why did you say that about angels?"

"It's just a saying we old folks have. We can't choose our time. When the angel of death comes calling, you have to go."

"Mrs. Adams, I saw it! I saw the angel! Calvin and I both saw it! It stopped outside our window this morning. It had its hand up like it was waving to us. Do you suppose it was Papa Joe?"

"Coulda' been, child. Coulda' been. It'd be just like Joe to make the angel stop so he could tell you goodbye. That's likely his way of letting you know he's got his wings and will keep watching over you."

The finality of his death hits me at his funeral. For once, Mama is sober. She's all dressed up and sitting with her sisters on the front pew. Calvin and I are behind her with the twins as close to me as they can get. Behind me, I hear the neighbors chatter back and forth as they wait for the service to start.

"Glennie cleans up all right when she has to," one

whispers.

"She's clean for the moment," another one titters, "but it won't last long. She'll be strung out again before Joe's in his grave."

"She was a good mother when Rosie was little. I don't know what happened, but she sure took a wrong turn."

Bad as Mama is, she is still our mother. They've got no business talking about her. I turn and glare indignantly at them, hoping they'll stop, but they don't notice.

"Seriously," the first one says, "look how close those little ones stick to Rosie."

"She's the only one they can stick to. Glennie's hardly ever home and she's plumb stoned when she is. Rosie's like a mother to them. I don't know how she keeps up in school, but according to the neighbor kids, she's on honor roll."

"Joe helped her whenever he could. He was so proud of her. He had big hopes for her future. He said she'll be a success at whatever she chooses to do."

"Well, she's got her hands full now. I don't know if she can manage Glennie without Joe dropping in to check on them."

It's odd. I feel totally, utterly alone but, at the same time, a glow of happiness radiates through me when I hear how much Papa Joe believed in me. My best friend in the whole world is gone. I won't let him down.

Chapter 20

Calvin Leaves

It's August already, almost time for school to start. I've got to find out how to get the twins registered for school. If I can get Calvin to watch the twins, I'll walk to school tomorrow and ask Mrs. Richmond.

Guess what?" I say to the twins. "In two weeks, you'll be in kindergarten."

"What's that?" Sophie wants to know.

"That's the very first grade in school. You'll ride the bus just like Rosie and Calvin and you won't have to stay home by yourselves any more. You'll learn how to read and write your name and you'll learn all the colors and numbers. You'll love it!"

I'm both excited and relieved. When they're in school, they'll get breakfast and lunch free. I won't need to worry about getting money to feed them.

All summer, Calvin has collected newspapers and the twins and I have scoured the park for aluminum cans to recycle. Even though he hates it, Calvin has watched the twins while I babysat to bring in extra money. When Mrs. Adams learned what we were doing, she arranged some ironing jobs for me so I could earn money at home. She showed me how to manage my money by shopping at the Farmer's Market and the day-old bread store. Each month, we've eked out enough to feed ourselves when Mama's welfare money ran out.

Mama hasn't changed. She occasionally has a good day, but usually she's drunk, drugged, and cantankerous. That's what Mrs. Adams calls her. I call her mean.

It's been a hard summer, but I'm proud of all we've done to stay together. That's why I'm totally unprepared for Calvin's announcement.

The twins are in bed and I'm sitting out on the porch. Calvin comes up the walkway and plops down beside me. "Sis, I'm leavin'."

"Wh-what do you mean?" I'm so dumbfounded I can hardly get the words out.

"I mean I'm outta here. I'm not going to live here anymore."

"Calvin! You can't be serious! I need you. I can't manage without you! We need every penny both of us are making to survive. I can't do it alone!"

"That's just the point, Sis. Look, I'm fourteen. You're almost thirteen. We spend all our time making money for food we shouldn't have to buy. If we're going to make money, we should at least be able to spend it on ourselves Do you have decent clothes to wear to school? No, except for the outfit Papa Joe got you, you've got nothing. Neither do I. These twins aren't our kids. I'm not going to take care of them for the rest of my life."

"Oh, that's just great!" I shout hysterically. "They're our brother and sister. You can't leave me here with all the responsibility. What if you were Anthony and your big brother left you? What would you do then, huh?"

Calvin doesn't answer and we fall into an angry

silence.

After a few minutes, he says, "Well, I'm going."

"Where are you going?"

"To Daddy Thompson's. He said I could come."

Calvin and I have different fathers. Daddy Thompson is Calvin's other grandfather.

"Did you tell him about us? Did you tell him we all need help?

"I mentioned y'all, but he said you being my sister doesn't make you his kin. Don't worry, Sis. My going will make one less mouth to feed. "

Calvin packs his few clothes into a paper bag and comes back to the porch. "See ya', Rosie. Tell Sophie and Anthony good-bye for me."

"Tell them yourself," I shout to his back as he walks off. "That's the least you can do!"

A deep, numbing chill settles over me, a feeling that nothing matters any more.

I'm so devastated I can't even cry. Once again, I'm staring at disaster. I go inside and lock the door. It's just the twins and me now, unless Mama comes home. Alone and afraid, I pace the darkened room, my stomach in a sick knot, screaming at God. "Why God, are you letting all this happen? What did I do to deserve this? You let Mama get on drugs and neglect us. I prayed for her to die and you let her live. I needed Papa Joe and you took him. Now Calvin's gone. Papa Joe said you love us. Well, I don't feel loved right now. How could you possibly love us and treat us this way?"

I don't realize I'm screaming out loud until Sophie and Anthony come padding out.

"What's wrong, Rosie?" Anthony wraps his tiny

arms around my leg and squeezes it. "Who're you mad at?"

Sophie snuggles in close. "It'll be all right, Rosie. We love you."

How can kids this little know just what to say? I'm still upset with Calvin and Mama and God, but I do love these guys.

I can almost hear Papa Joe saying, "It's time to shine, Rosie. These little ones need you."

I give them each a big hug. "Back to bed, guys. I have to be up early in the morning."

"Why? What's in the morning?"

"I'll tell you when you get up."

Chapter 21

I Confront Mama

Sunlight streaming into the room awakens me. I dash over to Mrs. Adams' house while the twins are still asleep.

"What're you doing up so early, Miss Deanna?"

"Mrs. Adams, I need a favor. Could you please watch Sophie and Anthony while I see how to get them in kindergarten?

'Your mama's not home?"

"No, Ma'am. Neither is Calvin."

"I'd watch them if I didn't have so many errands to run. How about I give you bus fare and you take them with you? It'll be good for them to see their school ahead of time."

"Oh, no, Ma'am! Mama won't allow us to accept charity. She'd be awfully mad if she knew I took money from you."

" I shouldn't say this, but your mama is the devil's own child. Not providing for your needs, but out doing what she wants all the time. Let me shut my mouth. Talking about your mama isn't going to solve your problem. Hmm. AJ told me once that you found money out on the street. Well, I expect you might find some more under that azalea bush in about half an hour."

I grin at her. "Mrs. Adams, I didn't know you were so sneaky."

"Sneaky? Didn't your mama teach you not to call old folks names? Why, if I ever heard AJ calling an old lady sneaky, I'd wear her out." Her eyes twinkle as she scolds.

"I'm sorry, Mrs. Adams, I didn't mean any harm."

"Go on now. If you don't hurry, it'll be too late to use whatever you find under that bush. The city bus will be by here in twenty minutes."

I sprint home. "Sophie! Anthony! Get up! We're going to school!" As they struggle into their clothes, I fix them each a slice of toast and a glass of juice. "Hurry! It's a long way!"

Passing the azalea bush just outside our door, I see the money Mrs. Adams has tucked between the branches.

"Wow! Look here! This is our lucky day! A five-dollar bill! If we hurry, we can catch the bus!" I should get an academy award for acting so surprised. From her porch, Mrs. Adams grins and waves.

Neither Sophie nor Anthony has ridden a bus before. In fact, they've never been anywhere except the park and Papa Joe's funeral.

At first, they cling to me, staring wide-eyed at the people around them. Then they press their noses against the window and soak in neighborhood sights they've never seen.

At school, I give them a guided tour of the classrooms, cafeteria, library, and playground before taking them to the office.

"Rosie," Sophie tugs at my shirt. "I don't want to come here." Her eyes are filled with tears and her chin is quivering.

"Why not, Sophie?"

"It's too big, I'll get lost."

I'm trying to console her when Ms. Richmond comes out of her office.

"Well, Deanna, who do we have here and why do we have tears?"

"Hi, Ms. Richmond. Sophie and Anthony are coming to kindergarten this year. Sophie's afraid she'll get lost."

Ms. Richmond sat down beside her. "Sophie, it is so nice to meet you. Deanna has told me about you and Anthony. I promise you won't get lost. Deanna never did and I'll bet you're as smart as she is. The teachers will take good care of you. Besides, you and Anthony have to watch out for each other. Let's dry your tears."

"Ms. Richmond, do I just bring them the first day or does Mama need to fill out some papers?"

"Your mother needs to complete these," she answers, handing me the registration forms. We'll also need their birth certificates, immunization records, and proof of address."

"What's an immunization record?"

"A record showing they've had their shots so they don't get communicable diseases. Have they had them?"

"I don't know. I don't think so."

"They need the first one before they can come to school. Deanna, why are you the one bringing the twins? Is everything all right at home?"

"It's about the same except Papa Joe died and Calvin left."

"Where'd Calvin go?" Anthony demanded anxiously. "Did he die too?"

If Calvin were here now, I think I'd strangle him. He has no idea how Anthony idolizes him.

"No, Anthony, he didn't die. He's at Daddy Thompson's. He might be back sometime."

"So you're alone?" Mrs. Richmond asked.

"We're doing all right," I answer evasively. The last thing I need is for the twins to tell Mama I said we're alone.

At that moment, the bus rounds the corner. Tucking the papers under my arm, I grasp each twin by a hand and hurry out to meet it.

Mama's home when we arrive. Anthony and Sophie are so excited they trip all over each other in their race to tell her about their adventure.

"Mama, we went to school. It's a big place."

"Sophie said she was afraid, but this nice lady said she'd take care of her so she wouldn't get lost."

"And we saw the room where we'll eat."

"Yeah, and we went on the bus," Anthony piped in. "We started to walk, but Rosie found some money by the big bush so we rode the bus. I never rode a bus before."

I tell Mama about the twins needing shots before they can start school and give her the paperwork to fill out.

A week later, the papers are still on the table, untouched. "Mama, school starts next week. The twins need their shots."

"I know when school starts and I don't need you to tell me my job!" Arguing won't help, so I back off. She's too out of it to even care if they get their shots.

Mama doesn't know me if she thinks I'm going to miss school this year. I'm determined the twins will be in school every day so I don't have to babysit. I start middle school this year. It'll be harder than elementary, but I am totally focused on my goals of going to college and getting out of the projects. I absolutely will not live like Mama.

Early the next morning, I wake the twins, split a banana with them, and head for the health department twenty blocks away. The temperature is in the high nineties. It doesn't take long for the sidewalk heat to sizzle its way through the twins' thin-soled shoes. I carry first one, then the other. Neither wants to be put down, but they're too heavy for me to carry both at once. We're thirsty and sweat-soaked by the time we arrive.

Judging from the line snaking out the door and down the block, we'll be here for hours. A few mothers are waiting under shade trees with their children.

A voice blares from the public address system, "Twenty-nine. Number twenty-nine."

One lady weaves her way toward the door, waving the number twenty-nine high above her head.

"Excuse me, Ma'am, where do I get a number? " I ask a bystander.

"At the receptionist's desk."

I grab the twins' hands and we form a human chain as we squeeze through the crowd, inching our way to the receptionist's window.

The receptionist, a tall, stern-faced lady, peers down at us over her half-glasses. "What do you want?"

"A number please. I brought my brother and sister to get their school shots. "

"Where's your mother?"

"She couldn't come. She's sick."

"Sorry, you have to have an adult with you."

"But they can't start school without their shots."

"That's right, but an adult needs to bring them. Next! Number thirty. Number thirty."

I'm angry, hot, frustrated, and discouraged. The way home seems twice as long. The temperature, according to the bank thermometer, is now over one hundred. By the time we reach home, I've made up my mind to have it out with Mama.

Worn out from the morning's long walk, the twins fall asleep on the couch. While they're sleeping, I run to Mrs. Adams' house.

"Where've you children been today? When I saw you light out of here early this morning, I thought to myself, 'Those children are sure going to be hot today.' It's a scorcher, isn't it? Just gettin' back home, aren't you. Where did you say you went?"

She is nosy, but somehow it feels good to have her caring about us. Busybody or not, I've come to depend on her.

"We went to the health department to get their school shots, but we couldn't get in without Mama."

"Wha-a-t! You children walked all that way in this sizzlin' hot weather for nothing? Why didn't you ask me for bus fare? Oh, that's right, you can't take charity. Does your mama know where you were? You could have been kidnapped being that far from home! My lord, my lord! Well, you're back safe. That's what matters."

"Mrs. Adams, I need advice."

"Of course, child, your own mama's not there for you to ask. What do you need, sweetie?"

"Where can I get school clothes for the twins? The only outfits they have are what they wore to Papa Joe's funeral and their shoes are all worn out."

"Well, we can't send them to school naked, can we? Think your mama would believe you if you were to find clothes under the azalea bush?" She cackled, enjoying her own joke. "You have any money left from your little jobs this summer?"

"Yes, Ma'am, I have a little."

"Tell you what, bring the twins tomorrow and we'll hit the thrift shops. They usually have good prices. AJ might have some hand-me-downs you could wear."

I'm waiting for Mama when she stumbles in about midnight. "Whachew doin' up?" Her slurred speech tells me she's been drinking.

"Waiting for you, Mama. We have to talk."

"We got nothin' to talk about." She lurches toward her bedroom, but I've been preparing for this talk all day. She's not going to bed until I've had my say.

"Oh, yes we do, Mama. Things are really bad here. Look, look in the refrigerator." I fling the door open so she can see its emptiness. "How about the cupboards? There's nothing there either. How do you expect us to live without food? I took the twins to get their shots today, but they couldn't get them unless you were there." Waving their school papers in her face, I rant at her, " Look, you haven't even bothered to fill out their papers. Mama, Papa Joe is dead. He can't help anymore. Calvin left and you have never once asked about him. It's just you, the twins, and me. I can't do everything myself. I need you to be the Mama again."

"You criticizin'me, girl? You think you're better'n your own mama? Where do you get off talkin'to me like I'm the child!" Her eyes are narrow slits and she spits her words out in a cold, challenging tone.

I don't back down.

"Mama, I'm telling you what we need. We need the old you back. The mama you were before you started boozing and shooting up. The one who used to help me with homework. The one who had dreams. The one who told me I could be anything I wanted to be if I worked hard. Mama, the twins never knew the old you. The only you they know is a drunken drug addict."

She goes into one of her coughing spasms. I can't tell if it's real or if she's hiding her feelings behind it. Finally, she speaks, her eyes soft with that faraway look they used to have when she was thinking of better things. "Rosie, I know I've failed you. I've failed myself. I thought if I sold drugs for just a little while, I could make enough money to get us out of here. I never planned to get hooked. I tried them once and thought I could stop. I always told you to stay away from them. I wish I'd listened to my own advice. You think it's too late for me to change?"

"Mama, I need you to try."

Chapter 22

A Ray of Hope

By some miracle, Mama stays sober long enough to get the twins' shots and complete all the school forms. On the Friday before school starts, I ask her to stay with the twins while I take their papers to the elementary school and pick up my schedule from the middle school.

On the way, I think about Mama. I believe her when she says she never meant to get hooked. I'm sorry I prayed for her to die. I guess anyone can make mistakes. I only wish hers weren't such big ones.

When I arrive at Oakland Park Elementary, the receptionist says, "Oh, Deanna, I'm glad you're here. Ms. Richmond wants to see you. Have a seat while I call her."

"What does she want?"

"She'll tell you."

"Is it good news or bad?" I try to get a hint of what it's about.

"Yes, it is," she teases.

"Yes, it is which?" I try again.

Ms. Richmond steps out from her office. "Come in, Deanna."

I'm shocked beyond words to see both Mrs. Bass and Mrs. Adams and am totally unprepared for what happens next.

"Deanna, Mrs. Bass and I have been discussing you since the day you first wrote your goals last year."

I look nervously at Mrs. Adams, wondering why she's here.

Ms. Richmond notices that I'm fidgeting, but she doesn't pause. "Your four goals were to learn everything you can, stay on honor roll, earn money, and go to college. Even though you had poor attendance, Mrs. Bass says you were her hardest working student last year. You studied hard while you were present and did your best to keep up when you were absent. Is that correct, Mrs. Bass?"

"Yes, it is. In fact, Deanna is the hardest working student I've ever had. Her work is high quality. If she keeps her grades up she should have no trouble getting into college."

"Ms. Richmond, I did work hard and I do want to go to college, but Tremayne and Lakeshia both helped a lot by making sure I had all the assignments."

"We know that. It's wonderful to have friends who care that much about you.

The point is you did the work even though you had some tough things going on at home.

You also met your second goal. Your records show that you've been on the A-B honor roll since first grade. With our tough standards, that's remarkable! Only about ten percent of our students have attained that status."

Hardly believing my ears, I interrupt. "The top ten percent? Are you sure? Oh, wow!"

The three of them, obviously enjoying my excitement, smile at each other.

"Your third goal was to earn money for college. You and Mrs. Bass talked about scholarships for outstanding students. She told you that people who make scholarship decisions look at many factors including grades, dependability, participation in school activities, and attendance."

"That's right, but why am I here? I've missed a lot of school and I'm not old enough for a scholarship. Kids don't get those until high school, do they?"

"Let's get first to why Mrs. Adams is here. The day you walked out on Ms. Walker, she told me that Mrs. Adams was aware of your situation and was keeping an eye on you and your family. When Mrs. Bass came across the news she's going to share, I called Mrs. Adams to get more information about you. She told me how hard you've worked to earn food money for your family, how you're almost totally responsible for the twins, and how your grandfather's death left you pretty much alone. Mrs. Adams told us you'd be here today and we invited her to meet with us.

"Now, Mrs. Bass, would you please tell Deanna what you've learned."

"Certainly. About a month ago, Deanna, the sixth grade teachers got information about a scholarship that will become available when you are a high school senior. The scholarship is for students who have an outstanding academic record, who want to go to college, and who have no financial possibility of going without a scholarship. I immediately thought of you. Each teacher could select one student from his or her class. Then we had to meet and narrow it down to just one student from each school. After hearing your story, all the sixth grade teachers and Ms. Richmond unanimously chose you. There are some criteria you'll have to meet. First, you have to improve your attendance record. Second, you have to maintain a B average for the next six years. Third, you have to score well on the Scholastic Aptitude Test. This scholarship will not pay all your college expenses, but it will help a lot."

They're all looking at me, waiting for a reaction. I am so absolutely stunned that I don't know what to say. I'm afraid if I say anything, I'll start crying. Except for Mrs. Adams helping me and Sophie and Anthony saying they love me, I can't think of anything good that has happened in a long, long time. Just the fact they thought of me is overwhelming.

"Y-You picked me out of all the sixth graders!" I stammer, fighting to swallow the lump in my throat. "Is this really happening to me?"

"Do you want to think about it for a while or shall we send your name in?" Ms. Richmond asks.

"Yes, I mean no. I mean, no, I don't want to think about it. Yes, send my name in. I can't believe this. Thank you, thank you, thank you! I won't disappoint you. I won't. With all that's happened with Mama and Papa Joe, I didn't think I'd ever get to college. Will I for sure get the scholarship if I do those things?"

"Yes," Mrs. Richmond answers, "it's for sure. I've already talked with the chairperson. For this year only, one student from each elementary school will be accepted. You're our selection."

I can feel a smile spreading over my face. In fact, I can't stop it. The more I sense freedom, the broader it gets.

Mrs. Adams chuckles, "Rosie, before you break your face with that big grin, there's something else you need to know. Your Papa Joe and I grew up together. He, your Grandma Rose, and I were best friends. As his first granddaughter, Joe insisted that you be named after his beloved Rose who died just before you were born. I never heard him call you Deanna. It was always Rosie. He loved you more than life itself and there wasn't anything he wouldn't do for his Rise and Shine Rosie. Before he died, he entrusted something to me. He asked me to keep it for you until you were grown. I think this would be a good time to show it to you. She hands me a photo album full of pictures of Papa Joe and Grandma Rose.

I hold it almost reverently as I turn the pages. He always said I resembled Grandma Rose. These pictures are proof of that.

"Thank you, Mrs. Adams. I'd be proud to have you hold it for me. With Mama acting like she does, there's no telling where we'll be living at any time. If you have it, I know it'll be safe."

"One more thing," she says, "before Joe died, he opened a one thousand dollar bank account in your name. His intention is that you use no more than one hundred dollars a year until you graduate. If you want to keep it all there until you go to college, you can do that. He set it up so that you and I would both have to sign for you to withdraw it. He trusted you to use it wisely, but he didn't want the rest of the family having access to it. In fact, he didn't want the rest of the family to know about it."

I sit there shaking my head in amazement. Three

adults who care about and believe in me just made it possible for me to realize my dreams and Papa Joe is still my guardian angel. I've never had such a gloriously, wonderful day.

"I'll make you all proud of me. I will. I promise."

Chapter 23

Another Disaster

I love middle school. The classes are challenging, but I'm working hard to keep my grades up. When things seem difficult, I repeat to myself, I've got a scholarship. I'm going to college. Nothing is going to stand in my way. I can do this.

Now that I have hope, I dream of getting a good job after college and of helping Sophie and Anthony if they want to go to college. I have no idea how much money that will take, but I'll help all I can. If they work hard, maybe they'll get scholarships too.

Mama's back to her old habits, working in the daytime, and drinking and shooting up at night. I don't worry about the twins because they're in school all day and Mrs. Adams watches them until I get home.

Life is better than it has been for a long time.

* * * * *

Just after the Christmas holiday, disaster strikes again.

It's a cold, dreary, rainy day – the kind that makes you want to stay inside and read. Although it's early afternoon, the streetlights are already on. Mrs. Adams has hot chocolate ready for AJ and me when we get off the bus.

During a brief lull in the rain, I hurry home with the twins. The instant we step into our dark duplex, a sickening odor tells me something is wrong.

Forgetting the cold, wet weather, I push Sophie and Anthony out to the porch. "You two wait here until I come get you. Don't move off this porch."

I turn on the lights.

"Mama, are you home? Mama?"

Silence answers me.

Her bedroom door is slightly ajar. Slowly, cautiously, I push it open and fumble for the light switch.

"No, Mama! No!" My stomach heaves in great contracting waves at the sight of Mama lying motionless on the floor, face down in her own vomit and blood. I clap my hand over my mouth, struggling to keep from throwing up.

A low moan tells me she's still alive. I check her pulse the way we were trained in health class. It's weak, but there. I turn her head so her face isn't in her vomit. Blood oozes from a gaping head wound onto the floor.

I'd like to say I'm calm, but I'm not. My legs are like jello as I grab the phone. My fingers are shaking so hard that I misdial 9-1-1. When I finally punch in the right numbers, my voice is shrill and my words are garbled.

A calm voice asks, "What is the nature of your emergency?"

"M-my mom! It's my mom. I th-think she's dying!"

"Is she able to tell you what's wrong?"

"No, she's unconscious."

"Is she still breathing? Does she have a pulse?"

"Yes, but it's weak. Hurry!"

"Can you describe her symptoms?"

"She's lying in vomit and there's blood all around her and when I turned her head, her eyes rolled back. Please, hurry!"

"An ambulance is on the way. Is there an adult there with you?"

"No, I mean yes. No, no one is here, but I can get my neighbor."

The twins! I forgot the twins! I drop the phone and rush out to the porch.

Grabbing each by a hand, I drag them frantically back to Mrs. Adams' house.

"Rosie, what's wrong? Why are we running?" Anthony asks.

"Mama's sick. An ambulance is coming to take her to the hospital."

"I wanna see Mama!" Sophie tries to pull away.

If Mama dies, I don't want them to remember her this way. They won't have many good memories as it is, but they don't need gross ones.

"No, Sophie, you're coming with me!"

"My lands, Rosie, what brings you back so soon?"

"Mrs. Adams, come quick! I need you!"

"Uh-oh. What's the trouble?"

"It's Mama! Please, hurry!"

"Goodness, Child, when you talk like that, I'm on the way! AJ, come out here and take care of these babies. Pronto!"

Sirens shriek through the late afternoon air as Mrs. Adams and I hurry across the street. Emergency vehicles screech to a halt by the curb. Paramedics jump from the ambulance and race with their gurney toward the house.

The police, with sirens blaring and lights flashing, arrive next. I recognize Sergeant Harris as he and his partner rush past me.

Mrs. Adams and I follow them into Mama's bedroom. Mrs. Adams takes one look at Mama and starts wailing, "Have mercy, have mercy! How much more can these poor dear children bear?" She tries to shield me from seeing what's happening, but my eyes are fixed on the awful scene.

"What in heaven's name happened here?" Sergeant Harris asks.

I'm so rattled I can hardly answer. "I-I-I d-don't know. I-I found M-Mama like this when I got home from school."

The paramedics, their shoes spattered with Mama's blood, work rapidly. Without pausing, one of them says, "From that nasty gash, it looks like she fell and banged her head on the corner of that dresser." Minutes later, they strap Mama onto the gurney and wheel her out the door.

"Little lady, you have someone to take care of you while your mama's in the hospital?" Sergeant Harris asks.

Before I can respond, Mrs. Adams puts her arm around my shoulder. I breathe a huge sigh of relief when I hear her say, "Yes, she does. I've not got much room, but I'll take them until their mama gets home. You've got no worries there."

As the paramedics load Mama into the ambulance, the neighbors, wrapped in heavy sweaters, gather on the sidewalk craning their necks for a better look.

Friday night, Aunt Dottie gets Calvin and takes us all to the hospital. She's not sure they'll let little kids in so we wait in the car while she goes to see Mama. When she comes back, Calvin and I will go in.

It's cold, so cold I can see my breath. The four of us snuggle together, but it's impossible to get warm. Aunt Dottie has been inside nearly half an hour when I decide we're going in. We'll all be sick if we don't.

We sit shivering in the hospital lobby. My toes and fingers tingle as warmth begins to creep into them. Calvin and I each have our arms wrapped around one twin.

None of us has been in a hospital since we were born. Looking down the long cavernous hallways extending from both sides of the lobby, I feel lost in its hugeness.

A large information desk fills the center of the lobby, but no one is there. I have no idea how to find Mama or Aunt Dot.

A kind-looking, tiny, red-haired lady in a pink uniform leaves the gift shop and approaches us, smiling. "You children look lost. Can I help you?"

My feeling of helplessness disappears. "I hope so," I answer. "We're here to see our Mama. She came in two days ago and we don't know how she is. We don't even know where she is."

"Just a minute, I'll find out for you." She goes to the computer. "What's her name?"

"Glennie Brown."

"Here she is. Room 427. Just get on the elevator by the drinking fountain and push button number 4.

When you get upstairs, someone will help you."

Being on an elevator is a new experience for us. We crowd together in one corner and wait, forgetting to push the button. Nothing happens until an old man gets in. "What floor?" he asks.

"Four."

"That's where I'm headed."

Fourth floor is a maze of peach colored walls going off in all directions. Instinctively, we grab hands and move as a single unit searching for Mama's room. Her door is open.

We step in expecting to see Aunt Dot. She isn't here. Mama isn't either. What I mean is, she's lying there with her eyes closed, but it's like she's not inside her body or else she's so deep inside, she doesn't know we're here. In a huddled mass, we inch closer to the bed. I touch Mama's arm. It is so, so cold. She doesn't respond.

The twins stare wide-eyed at the white-blanketed figure. Sophie speaks first. "Rosie, where's Mama?"

I know I shouldn't have bought them here. "That is Mama. She's very sick."

"Will she get better?"

"I don't know, Sophie."

I don't think she will, but I don't want to scare Sophie and Anthony. A myriad of thoughts and feelings flit through my mind: guilt for having prayed for Mama's death, fear and uncertainty about what will happen to us if she dies. I often wanted Mama dead, but I never thought about how final death is and the changes it would bring.

I look at the person lying there and think of the

good times we once had. Then I remember the cruel, uncaring person she had become. I recall the conversation we had when she thought she could stop using drugs. I think about the way she has failed all of us, including herself. Memories of all the nights we were left alone, the locked doors, the days without food, the switchblade at my throat, and the lonely, joyless Christmases flood over me. The mama I once loved died a long time ago. The person lying here is the stranger she became. There's no point in staying.

Chapter 24

Death and Separation

Mrs. Adams and AJ are waiting in the kitchen when we return. A knowing look passes between them and, as if by a pre-arranged signal, AJ whisks the twins off to bed. When Mrs. Adams wraps her arms around me in a long, hard hug, I know Mama is dead.

"She's gone, isn't she?"

"Yes, Rosie, she is. She died right after you left."

"Mrs. Adams, I don't understand. How could she die from a fall?"

Mrs. Adams closes her eyes and takes a deep breath. "Deanna, the only way to deal with bad news is to come out with it. Your mama lost a lot of blood when she fell, but she didn't die from the fall alone. She was very sick. That cough she had was a symptom of AIDS. She probably got it from using needles."

There's a hard, heavy lump in my heart. I feel like I'm expected to cry, but I can't.

"Mrs. Adams, I know this sounds awful, but it came to me in the hospital that Mama died a long time ago. All she did tonight was stop breathing."

Mrs. Adams pulls away and peers at me over her wire-rimmed glasses. "Goodness, Child, your thinking is too deep for this old brain. You're right, of course."

"What will happen to us now? Who will keep us?"

"I don't know, darlin'. I'd keep you if I could, with

you and AJ being such good friends, but we have only the two tiny bedrooms. The twins can sleep on the floor and you on the sofa for a few nights, but that's not a good permanent arrangement. There, there, I'm rambling again. You'll stay here until Ms. Walker finds a place for you."

"Do you think the twins and I will get to stay together?"

"I hope to the good Lord you can. Goodness knows they need you. With Papa Joe, Glennie, and Calvin all gone, it doesn't seem right that you'd be separated. You've been like a mama to them almost since they were born."

The next morning, I take the twins to the playground. The air is crisp and chilly, but the sun is out and the temperature is starting to rise. I watch them come squealing down the slide, giggling as they crawl through the play tunnels, and playfully pushing each other off the balance beam. Painfully aware that I may never get to bring them here again, I struggle to find a way to tell them about Mama.

Worn out at last, they come panting and puffing to sit with me on the bench.

We sit here quietly, the three of us. After a few minutes, Anthony pipes up, "Mama didn't talk to us last night. When is she going to get better and come home?"

"She can't come see us anymore. She died, like Papa Joe did."

Sophie's soft brown eyes look into mine. "Is she an angel like Papa Joe?"

"I don't know, Sophie."

"Who will take care of us?"

"I don't know that either."

"When can we go home?" I wish Sophie wouldn't ask so many questions because I don't have the answers.

"We can't live there anymore. We can get our things, but we can't live by ourselves without an adult."

"What's a 'dult?" Anthony wants to know.

"It's a grown-up, a mom or dad or grandparent, who can take care of us."

"But Rosie, we haven't had any 'dults for a long time. You been takin' care of us. Why can't you still?"

"The Child Welfare Agency will say I'm too young. It would be great if someone would take all of us, but people don't usually have room for three extra children."

It's a somber trio that arrives at Mrs. Adams' house just in time to hear her screeching into the telephone. "What! You can't mean that! Why that's the most hardhearted, calloused thing I've ever heard! The poor woman just died last night. Yes, yes, I've done the best I could, but you need to have it professionally cleaned. No one will want to live there with those bloodstains on the floor. You want things cleaned out when? By Wednesday? That's just four days away! You miserable penny-pinching slumlord!"

Muttering angrily, she bangs the receiver down and slams her chair in place against the table. That's when she sees us staring speechlessly at her.

"Land sakes' alive! I didn't know you children were back. I'm sorry you heard me calling names and getting so upset. Talk about the almighty dollar! That miser can't even wait for the dead to be buried before renting your home to someone else!"

We're getting our clothes from the duplex when Aunt Dottie and her boyfriend, Jermaine, drive up. "What are you doing in my sister's home?" she questions Mrs. Adams. "You've got no right to be here. Nothing here belongs to you."

"Have mercy, Miss Dot, I don't want anything. I just brought the children to get some of their belongings. More'n likely Calvin will want to get his things, too."

"Well, if it ain't my boss lady," Jermaine drawls as he watches Ms. Walker pull up by the curb.

"Comin' to check on the deceased?" he asks, as she arrives at the door.

"What are you doing here, Jermaine?"

"I'm here with Glennie's sister to keep folks from taking her belongings. Looks like we arrived just in time." He stares at Mrs. Adams as he says it.

Suddenly, it all makes sense. Jermaine works in Ms. Walker's office. He has to be the one who warned Mama about Ms. Walker's visits.

"Jermaine, it was you!" I say accusingly. "You're the one who told Mama every time Ms. Walker was coming. If it weren't for you, Mama could have been helped. For sure, she'd still be alive. You helped ruin her life and now you have the nerve to come in this house and say Mrs. Adams is taking things! Get out! Get out now!"

"Girl," Jermaine sneers, "I have no idea what you're talking about, but I don't think a child can throw a social worker out."

Ms. Walker glares stonily at him. "I'll talk with you

later. Right now, I need to meet with Rosie and Dot and Mrs. Adams."

Within the hour, it's decided that the twins will stay with Aunt Dottie, who makes it clear she has no room for me. I'm not a mind reader, but I'm sure she doesn't trust Jermaine around me."

I follow Ms. Walker to her car. "Ms. Walker, can't you please find a place for the three of us to stay together? The twins have been through a lot. They need me."

"Deanna, I'm sure you're correct about that being the best thing, but we try to keep children with relatives. The twins will be together. At least, we're not separating them. I'll find a placement for you as soon as possible. In the meantime, you'll all stay with Mrs. Adams until after the funeral."

"Ms. Walker, don't you get it? Jermaine is not a nice man! He had to be the one who told Mama when you were coming! Not only that, I stayed there for a few weeks and there's a reason Aunt Dottie doesn't want me there. I don't want anything to happen to Sophie, if you know what I mean."

"Deanna, first, we have no proof Jermaine is the one who notified your mother and frankly, with her gone, it would be impossible to prove. Secondly, there's a big difference between you and Sophie. For one thing, you're almost a woman and she's just a little child. I don't think you have to worry. I promise I'll check often."

No amount of begging, cajoling, or reasoning will change Ms. Walker's mind.

After everyone has gone, I go back into our duplex.

Sitting in the cold darkness, I reflect on the way my life has changed in the last year and a half and wonder what to do next. I don't want to live just anywhere. I want to be near the twins. I need them as much as they need me.

Suddenly, I remember Ms. Richmond once gave me her phone number and told me to call if I ever needed help. This definitely qualifies as one of those times. I rummage through my dresser drawer until I find her number. Her phone rings and rings and rings. Please be home. Please, please, please! I need to talk to someone. I'm about to hang up when she answers.

"Ms. Richmond, this is Deanna Rose Blakely. You said I could call you if I needed help and I need it."

"What's wrong, Deanna?"

"Everything is wrong. I thought if Mama died, things would be better so I prayed for her to die. Last night, she did and everything got worse." My voice shakes at the realization of how desperate my situation is. Gulping down the lump in my throat, I continue. "The landlord wants us out of the house by next week so he can rent it to someone else. Aunt Dottie is taking the twins, but says there's no room for me. Mrs. Adams doesn't have any room either. Ms. Walker says she'll find me a place, but I don't want to be in a foster home with strangers. I'd probably never get to see the twins and I couldn't bear that. They're all I have! Ms. Richmond, can I come live with you? I wouldn't cause any problems and I know you'd let me see my brother and sister."

I can't believe the words I hear coming from my mouth. When I called Ms. Richmond, I never even thought of asking if I could live with her. I just needed to talk with someone. If the long pause after my question is any indication, I think I took her by surprise. I so much want her to say yes and I'm terrified that she won't. My insides are tense as I hold my breath waiting for her answer.

"I am so sorry to hear about your mother, Deanna. I know you had difficult times with her, but the fact you reported her tells me you cared about her and wanted her to change. Where are you staying now?"

"I'm staying with Mrs. Adams until after the funeral. I don't know where I'll go after that," I answer wistfully.

"When is the funeral?"

"Wednesday, four days from now. I'd like for you to come, if you can. It would mean a lot to have someone there who cares about me."

"More people care about you than you know, Deanna. I'll try to come. In the meantime, help Mrs. Adams all you can with the twins. It's hard for someone her age to take care of little children."

I notice she didn't answer my question, but at least she didn't say no.

Chapter 25

Rise and Shine, Rosie

In the days before the funeral, I make sure the twins are in school. I want life to be as normal as possible for them. Afternoons and evenings, I spend every spare minute with them. Knowing we'll soon be separated, I soak up every smile, every word.

In the meantime, I wait to hear from Ms. Richmond.

Hundreds of people came to Papa Joe's funeral. Only the family, Mrs. Adams, AJ, Ms. Richmond, and Mrs. Bass come to Mama's. Papa's Joe's funeral lasted two hours; Mama's, twenty minutes. At Papa Joe's funeral, people talked about all the good he had done. At Mama's, the preacher speaks about the evils of strong drink and drugs.

After the service, everyone comes back to Mrs. Adams' house. Ms. Walker is there to supervise the twins' move to Aunt Dottie's.

Aunt Dot is in a hurry to leave. I think she's worried the twins will make a scene. "Come on, Sophie. Get your things, Anthony. We've got to get home. I've got things to do."

My heart breaks when Sophie says, "Come on, Rosie. Let's go."

Doing my best not to cry, I kneel down and give her a long, hard hug. "Sweetie, Rosie's not coming.

Aunt Dottie doesn't have room for all of us, but I want you to be really good for Aunt Dot. Do everything she says and remember, I'll always love you."

"You love me too, Rosie?" Anthony snuggles in for his hug.

"Yes, Anthony! I love you, too."

"Where will you live?" Sophie asks.

My eyes brim with tears and my mouth fights contortions as I give them one last hug.

"I don't know. When I find a place, I'll let you know."

Mrs. Bass steps forward. "Deanna, Ms. Richmond said you asked to stay with her. She doesn't have any extra room, but I do. I've talked with my family about your situation. If you'd like and if Ms. Walker approves, you are welcome to stay with us. The twins can visit as often as you wish if it's okay with your Aunt Dottie."

Tears of relief spurt from my eyes and run down my cheeks as I jump excitedly to my feet. "Do you mean it? Do you really, really mean it? Oh, thank you! Thank you for giving me a chance! I won't be any trouble, I promise."

Sometimes, when I lie in bed at night in my new home, I think about all that has happened. I've achieved my dream of getting out of the projects and I'm never going back, except of course, to visit Mrs. Adams and my friends. I think about my future, about going to college and getting a good job. I dream of being reunited with Sophie and Anthony when they get older. I think of Papa Joe. Every night, I tell him, "Papa Joe, I'm your Rise and Shine Rosie and I won't disappoint you."

Even though he's gone, I can almost hear him

whisper, "I know, Rosie, I know."